Other Books by Harriet Steel

Becoming Lola

Salvation

City of Dreams

Following the Dream

Dancing and Other Stories

The Inspector de Silva Mysteries

Trouble in Nuala

Dark Clouds over Nuala

Offstage in Nuala

Fatal Finds in Nuala

Christmas in Nuala

Passage from Nuala

Rough Time in Nuala

Taken in Nuala

High Wire in Nuala

Cold Case in Nuala

Break from Nuala

Stardust in Nuala

AN INSPECTOR DE SILVA MYSTERY

LONG ODDS
IN NUALA

HARRIET STEEL

Author's Note and Acknowledgments

Welcome to the thirteenth book in the Inspector de Silva mystery series. Like the previous ones, this is a self-contained story but wearing my reader's hat, I usually find that my enjoyment of a series is deepened by reading the books in order and getting to know major characters well. With that in mind, I have included thumbnail sketches of those taking part in this story who have featured regularly in the series.

Several years ago, I had the great good fortune to visit the island of Sri Lanka, the former Ceylon. I fell in love with the country straight away, awed by its tremendous natural beauty and the charm and friendliness of its people. I had been planning to write a detective series for some time and when I came home, I decided to set it in Ceylon in the 1930s, a time when British Colonial rule created interesting contrasts, and sometimes conflicts, with traditional culture. Thus Inspector Shanti de Silva and his friends were born.

I owe a debt of gratitude to everyone who helped with this book. John Hudspith was as usual an invaluable editor. Julia Gibbs did a marvellous job of proofreading the manuscript, and Jane Dixon Smith designed another excellent cover and layout for me. Sarah and Julian Richmond Watson very kindly shared some of their knowledge of the world of racing with me. My thanks also go to all those readers who have told me they enjoyed the previous books in the series and would like to know what Inspector de Silva and his friends did next. Their enthusiasm has encouraged me to keep writing. Above all, my heartfelt gratitude goes to my husband Roger for his unfailing encouragement and support, to say nothing of his patience when Inspector de Silva's world distracts me from this one.

Apart from well-known historical figures, all characters in this book are fictitious. Nuala is also fictitious although loosely based on the hill town of Nuwara Eliya. Any mistakes are my own.

Characters who appear regularly
in the Inspector de Silva Mysteries

Inspector Shanti de Silva. He began his police career in Ceylon's capital city, Colombo, but in middle age he married and accepted a promotion to inspector in charge of the small force in the hill town of Nuala. He likes a quiet life with his beloved wife, his car, good food, and his garden. He dislikes interference in his work by his British masters and formal occasions.

Jane de Silva. She came to Ceylon as a governess to a wealthy colonial family and met and married Shanti de Silva a few years later. A no-nonsense lady with a dry sense of humour, she likes detective novels, cinema, and dancing.

Sergeant Prasanna. In his early thirties and married with a daughter. He is doing well in his job and taking increasing responsibility. He likes cricket and is exceptionally good at it.

Constable Nadar. A little younger than Prasanna. Diffident at first, he has gained in confidence over the years. He is married with two boys and likes making toys for them.

Archie Clutterbuck. The British assistant government agent in Nuala and as such responsible for administration and keeping law and order in the area. He is devoted to his Labrador retriever, Darcy, and enjoys fishing and golf. He dislikes being argued with, and the heat.

Florence Clutterbuck. Archie's wife, a stout, forthright lady. She likes to be queen bee and organise other people.

Doctor David Hebden. Doctor for the Nuala area. Under his professional shell, he is rather shy. He likes cricket and dislikes formality.

Emerald Hebden (née Watson). She arrived in Nuala with a touring British theatre company, decided to stay and subsequently married David Hebden. She is a popular addition to local society and a good friend to Jane. Her full story is told in *Offstage in Nuala*.

Sanjeewa Gunesekera. The manager of the best hotel in Nuala, the Crown, and an old friend of Shanti de Silva.

George Appleby. The local veterinary surgeon and the government veterinary adviser for the Nuala area. Married with a large family, he is a well-liked man. Rose Appleby is his eldest daughter.

PROLOGUE

Late autumn, 1941

Excitement tinged with apprehension gripped Rose Appleby as she drove her little Austin up the road that led from town to Nuala's racecourse. She was heading for the livery yard attached to the course where she stabled her bay mare, Slipper. The sun was newly risen, its slanting rays spreading across the hills that surrounded the town, the outlines of the course's grandstand and its surrounding buildings emerging from darkness. Rose slowed to pass a group of men walking down the hill from the direction of the course – she guessed they were night watchmen who had finished their duties – then she speeded up again to cover the last quarter of a mile.

Two cars were parked in the yard outside the racecourse's office. A light glowed in one of the windows, and she saw a shadowy figure move across it. She wondered if it was Edmund Fallowfield, the secretary of the Nuala Jockey Club, the organisation that owned the racecourse. On the occasions when she'd come up to the stables early, she'd often noticed that he was already at work. No doubt there was even more than usual to do on such an important day. On the other hand, as far as she was aware, neither of the cars was his. He drove a Hillman. But perhaps that was at the garage, and today he'd borrowed one.

She parked to the left of the cars and climbed out. That morning she had dressed hurriedly in a pair of old jodhpurs, a white short-sleeved Aertex shirt and her old brown leather riding boots, but at home a pair of smart new jodhpurs and her purple and yellow jockey's silks hung on the door of her bedroom wardrobe. This was going to be a momentous day. For the first time in Nuala's history, the Hill Country Cup meeting, the most important one in the town's racing calendar, was to include a ladies' race. Six amateur lady jockeys had entered, and she was one of them.

The way to Slipper's stable passed by the archway into the yard where the looseboxes attached to the racecourse were situated. They were used when horses had been ridden up to the course the day before their race and needed somewhere to be stabled overnight. Rose paused, noticing a young man she didn't recognise emerge from beneath the archway. He looked to be in a hurry and although she called out a good morning and was close enough for him to have heard it, he didn't acknowledge her. She felt a little peeved; young men didn't usually ignore her, but she shrugged and walked on.

As she reached the livery yard, she heard loud banging sounds and raised an eyebrow. It was probably Rupert Wilde's black stallion, Sultan. The horse had a habit of trying to kick down the door of his loosebox. Still to make his racing debut, he was a handsome beast, but unpredictable – a dangerous trait in such a large and powerful animal. Even the boldest of the stable lads avoided him whenever they could. From what she'd seen and heard of his owner Rupert, thought Rose, he was probably best avoided too. He was an incorrigible flirt and far too pleased with himself for her liking. She had no desire to become another of his conquests.

Apart from Sultan, who at intervals continued to hammer at his loosebox door, the horses in the yard drowsed. There was no sign of Sunil, the stable lad who usually looked after Slipper. Rose frowned. He'd promised he would come up early, but perhaps he'd overslept. She went over to Slipper's box and the mare greeted her with a low whinny. Rose stroked her soft, silky cheek and inhaled the earthy aromas of horse and straw.

'Hello, lady,' she murmured. 'We'll show them how it's done today, won't we?'

Slipper tossed her head as if she understood and Rose laughed. 'That's right, my angel.'

Footsteps sounded behind her, and she turned to see Sunil. He gave her one of his lopsided grins. 'Good morning, Missy Rose.'

'Ah, there you are, Sunil. I thought you'd be here when I arrived. Where have you been?'

The grin vanished and Sunil hesitated then he mumbled something inaudible and turned his head away, avoiding her eyes like a dog that feared a whipping. Rose cursed herself for asking. Sunil was often in a world of his own. She ought to know by now that he became distressed if he thought he was being asked to account for himself or told off. She must be more nervous about today's race than she'd realised to have forgotten that. 'Never mind,' she said quickly. 'You're here now. Why don't you fetch Slipper some water?'

Like the sun coming out from behind a cloud, the grin returned. Sunil hurried off and soon returned with a filled tin bucket. Rose stood aside to give him room to carry it into the loosebox. There was a splash as the water poured into the stone trough on the back wall.

'Today's going to be exciting, isn't it,' said Rose when he came out again, fastening the bottom half of the loosebox door behind him.

'We'll win, won't we, Missy Rose?' Sunil put down the bucket and clapped his hands.

'I hope so, but we mustn't count our chickens before they hatch.'

Sunil stroked Slipper's neck and she stretched out her head to nuzzle his shoulder.

'Shall I groom her, Missy Rose?'

Slipper's coat already gleamed, but Rose knew it was a job that Sunil loved.

'That's a good idea.'

Sunil beamed and started out for the tack room then stopped abruptly as Edmund Fallowfield came into the yard. He paused for a few moments to speak to Sunil then Sunil scurried away.

Fallowfield came to join Rose. 'Poor fellow, it's always hard to get a word out of him. Do you know if there's some problem?'

'No,' said Rose quickly. 'It's just that he's shy.' She didn't want to discuss Sunil with Fallowfield. He might form the inference that Sunil wasn't up to his work.

'Our head lad, Anishka, speaks very highly of the lad's way with the horses.' Fallowfield tapped his forehead with one finger. 'It's unfortunate he's not quite right up here.'

'It's through no fault of his own.'

'Of course not. I assure you that if I have anything to do with it, allowances will be made.'

'I hope so.'

'Then I'll do my best to ensure you're not disappointed.' Fallowfield gave her a warm smile. 'Talking of Anishka, have you seen him this morning?'

Rose shook her head. 'I'm afraid not.'

'If you do, I'd be grateful if you'd tell him I need a word. I'll be in my office.'

'I'll tell him.'

Out of the corner of her eye, Rose saw Sunil returning with the grooming equipment. Fallowfield gave him an encouraging smile. 'Excellent. We like the horses to look their best on Cup day. Well, I'll leave you to continue with the good work. And I wish you the best of luck in your race, Miss Appleby.'

'Thank you, Mr Fallowfield.'

After he'd gone, she stayed with Sunil and Slipper for a little while, watching as the stable lad diligently brushed and polished the mare's coat, then went back to her car to go home for breakfast. As she was about to drive off, Edmund Fallowfield put his head out of his office door. He smiled broadly and waved, and she waved back, but privately she felt a twinge of irritation. She hoped he wasn't developing a crush on her. He was probably a nice man but not her type and a lot older than her anyway.

She felt a little sorry for him though. He'd only come to work at the racecourse a few months ago, and unlike Pat Masham, who was in charge of the staff who worked at the livery stables and helped out with the horses that came up for race meetings, or Peter Findley, the clerk of the course, he never seemed entirely at ease with the members of the Jockey Club. It was a feeling with which she could sympathise. Some of them were perfectly pleasant but there were many who made little effort to hide their disapproval of a woman who wanted to enter the racing world, even if it was only as an amateur. Her eyes narrowed. She had no intention, however, of letting *that* put her off.

CHAPTER 1

The de Silvas arrived at the racecourse at midday and went to find their friends, the local doctor David Hebden and his wife Emerald, at the place where they'd agreed to meet. A table covered with a white cloth was already set up under the shade of a small canopy and two of the Hebdens' house servants were laying out a picnic. De Silva looked with interest at the selection of packages, boxes, and bowls. He hoped something more appetising than that British apology for lunch, the sandwich, was going to come out of them. His mind went back to the comical description of the picnic in *The Wind in the Willows*, a story that, as a child, he had never tired of his mother reading to him. It was strange how one's early memories could be so vivid and precise. Some people said they were often more so than what had happened yesterday.

Emerald was busy directing the picnic operations, so her husband saw them first and waved. 'Good afternoon! Come and sit down and have something cold to drink. You must be hot after the drive up here. We thought we'd eat our picnic then take a stroll over to the paddock to see the parade of horses entered in the ladies' race.'

'That sounds lovely,' said Jane, sitting down in the chair Hebden had pulled out for her. She smiled as her god-daughter, the Hebdens' little girl Olivia, dressed in a pale blue smock and a sunhat of soft white straw, scampered in her direction. Jane reached down to give her a hug and Olivia scrambled onto her lap and started to play with the sapphire brooch that Jane wore.

'Do be careful, Olivia,' said Emerald. 'You might break it.'

'Oh, I'm sure she wouldn't do that.'

'I wouldn't count on it,' said David Hebden cheerfully. 'She was sitting on my lap yesterday evening looking at one of her picture books, and she tweaked my nose so hard that my eyes watered. Small children don't know their own strength.'

'I hope you don't mind us bringing her,' said Emerald.

'Of course we don't, do we, Shanti?'

'Certainly not.'

'David and I thought she'd enjoy seeing the horses and of course, she loves a picnic. But if she gets tired and starts to grizzle, ayah will stay here with her so that she can take a nap.'

An hour passed very pleasantly as they chatted and sipped cool lemonade, enjoying the picnic which turned out to include sandwiches but also, to de Silva's relief, various spicy snacks, fresh fruit, cheese, and a large fruit cake – a British delicacy to which he was very partial. After he had polished off a second slice, he sat back in his chair replete.

'Well, are we all ready for a walk to the paddock?' asked Hebden.

De Silva grinned. 'I think I can just about move. Thank you, the picnic was delicious.'

Emerald decided that it would be too far for Olivia to walk so, much to her delight, Hebden swung her up on his shoulders, and they set off.

'Quite an occasion today,' he remarked as he and de Silva fell into step behind their wives. 'The first time a ladies' race will be run here and on the same day as the most prestigious one in Nuala's racing calendar.'

'Jane is of the opinion that it's about time.'

Hebden nodded. 'Emerald says much the same. I see from the race card that the prize money for the Hill Country Cup is a hundred guineas, but of course it's far less for the ladies' race, and the jockeys will be amateurs rather than professionals as they are in the Cup. All the same, I'm sure it will be a splendid event.' He reached up to shift Olivia's position on his shoulders. 'You're getting heavy, young lady.'

The racecourse had become crowded in the past hour, and everyone was dressed in their best. For the local ladies it was brightly coloured saris embellished with intricate embroidery and for their menfolk smart tunics and loose trousers. Most of the British ladies were dressed as colourfully as their local counterparts but with the addition of hats. These were obviously an opportunity to let their wearers' imagination have free rein. Feathers, bows, braid, tulle, and bunches of artificial flowers were all in evidence.

As usual, there were many food stalls selling spicy snacks as well as fruit, from slices of mango and scarlet watermelon to pomegranates and the evil smelling durian fruit which tasted so much better than it smelled. Not wanting his friend to think that he was still hungry after the picnic, de Silva resisted temptation.

Fortune tellers were also plentiful. Belief in clairvoyance was deeply ingrained in most people born in Ceylon and many liked to consult a fortune teller before significant events in their lives, including placing a bet, particularly if it was a large one. De Silva didn't regard himself as superstitious, but he wasn't immune to the instinct. Today, however, he decided to risk a few rupees without such assistance.

A considerable number of people were lining the paddock's railings, but the Hebdens and the de Silvas managed to find a place. Hebden lifted Olivia off his shoulders and held her in his arms, pointing to the six horses and riders circling the paddock. The horses' coats gleamed in the sunshine and the jockeys' bright silks outshone even the vivid green of the grass.

'There, what do you think of that?' he asked.

'Efelants!' squeaked Olivia. 'Efelants!'

Hebden laughed. 'No, my love, they're horses, not elephants. They have no trunks and they're considerably smaller. And less dangerous, thank goodness, or we wouldn't be standing so close.'

'Has she seen elephants?' asked Jane.

'Only in a picture book,' said Emerald. 'Luckily, they've never invaded our garden as they have some people's.'

'I'm glad we can say the same. Florence once told me they'd done a lot of damage at the Residence. Tearing branches off some of their lovely trees and trampling over flowerbeds.'

'I suppose it's the penalty of living in a country where one's often so close to nature,' observed Hebden. 'Something people are almost out of the habit of in many countries.'

Mounted on Slipper, Rose Appleby passed close to where they were standing. She smiled at the Hebdens, and they wished her good luck. 'Who was that?' asked de Silva as she and her mount moved on. She was a remarkably pretty young woman. He was surprised he hadn't noticed her before at any of the town's gatherings.

'Why, she's the Applebys' eldest daughter, Rose,' said Emerald. 'She's just turned eighteen, so the rules allow her to enter the race. She recently finished her education down at the British school for girls in Colombo, so she's living at home full-time now. Her mother told me she's just started work as a junior reporter on the *Nuala Times*.'

De Silva knew that Emerald was well acquainted with the Appleby family and had even lived with them for a while before her marriage. Presumably that was why she was well informed about their daughter. He studied Rose's profile as she reached the side of the paddock opposite them. He saw the resemblance to Mrs Appleby now: the fair hair, high cheekbones, and retroussé nose, but it looked as if the daughter had more of a hint of mischief to her. Over the years, the Applebys and their large brood of children had become a familiar sight at gatherings in Nuala, but he had never really distinguished one from another. So, this was their eldest daughter, turned into a young woman, and a very pretty one at that. It made him feel old.

'She must be a good rider to participate in this race,' he remarked.

'Oh, she is. She was always a tomboy and not afraid of anything. Independent minded. She was full of mischief when she was growing up. She gave her parents quite a few headaches, I can tell you.'

He guessed that a young lady in possession of good looks and a lively personality wouldn't go unnoticed by the young men of Nuala. To bear out his theory, a rumbustious group hung over the paddock railings vying to talk to her. They wore the usual cream suits of the Englishman in the tropics, but their appearance was enlivened by a selection of fancy waistcoats and brightly coloured ties.

'Rose always attracts a lot of attention,' said Emerald with a smile.

Parade completed, the horses and their jockeys filed out of the paddock and headed for the start.

'Well, if any of us are going to place a bet, now's the time,' said Hebden.

'Shall we have one?' asked Emerald. 'I think that we should as it's Rose, and Slipper looks such a beautiful horse. I do hope they win.'

Jane looked at de Silva. 'It would be fun to put on a small bet.'

'I agree it will make the race more interesting.'

'Shall we go and see to that, de Silva?' asked Hebden. He put Olivia down. 'I'd better leave her with you, Emerald. It's

11

bound to be crowded around the bookmakers' stalls. Shall we meet afterwards at the entrance to the grandstand?'

As their husbands disappeared into the crowd, Jane and Emerald looked at Olivia. She was rubbing her eyes and clenching a fistful of the skirt of Emerald's flower-patterned red dress in her pudgy little hands. 'Perhaps we should take her back to ayah,' said Emerald. 'She's seen the horses, and it might be better for her to have a rest rather than watch the race. All the noise might frighten her.'

She scooped Olivia up and they walked back to where they had eaten their picnic. The remnants of the meal had been cleared away and only the ayah and two of the servants were there.

'David told the servants they could go and watch the racing,' said Emerald. 'As long as they took it in turns.'

Olivia's thumb had crept into her mouth. Emerald handed her to her ayah, then she and Jane set off for the grandstand where they waited for de Silva and Hebden to join them. They arrived a few minutes before the race, and all found a place to sit.

On the course, the horses and jockeys were up at the starting line, milling around as they waited for the starter to fire the gun. De Silva always thought it was a miracle that racehorses didn't bump into each other when that happened. It seemed impossible to arrange them beforehand in a neat line but somehow, they managed to put themselves in order once they set off.

'The odds are pretty long on Slipper,' said Hebden. 'Twenty to one. In fact, none of the horses have very short odds. I suppose there's never been a race like this before so it's hard to predict how the riders will shape up. I believe they're all good, and most of them have competed in point-to-points and pony club events, but today they might suffer more from nerves as it's such a big event.'

At the crack of the starting gun, all eyes turned to the

course. The horses were to make a full circuit of the track before entering the final furlong to the finishing post in front of the box where the members of the Royal Nuala Jockey Club and other dignitaries had taken their seats. De Silva had already noticed that his boss, Archie Clutterbuck, the assistant government agent, and Archie's wife Florence were amongst them.

At first the six horses stayed bunched together, surging down the course like a multi-coloured wave rushing to shore. Gradually, however, the gaps between them widened. The murmur of the crowd grew louder as two horses took the lead. David Hebden lowered his binoculars. 'I'm afraid Slipper's only in fourth place,' he said. 'The bookies won't pay out on that.'

Emerald took his arm. 'There's still a fair way to go. I wouldn't be surprised if Rose isn't holding Slipper back to let the others set the pace.'

Hebden smiled. 'I didn't know you were a racing expert, my love.'

'I'm not, but Rose's father George, who follows racing, was telling me that's often how it's done.'

As the horses entered the final furlong, one of the ones at the rear began to move up. David Hebden put his binoculars to his eyes once more and fiddled with the dial that controlled the focus. 'Well, I'll be damned if it isn't Slipper!'

'There,' said Emerald. 'What did I tell you!'

The commentator's voice, heard through the persistent crackle of the racecourse's ageing loudspeaker system, rose until it was at fever pitch. 'It's number four, Slipper, ridden by Rose Appleby! Moving up into third place and still gaining ground!'

The crowd was buzzing with excitement, and despite the fact that he was no great racing fan, de Silva felt it too – a tightening in the stomach that spread to his chest and clamped it in an iron band. With the free hand that wasn't holding his race card, he gripped the white rail in front of him.

'Rags to Riches in the lead. Slipper in second place!' shouted the commentator. 'But Slipper's still moving up!'

De Silva saw Rose hunch lower in the saddle, head down into the wind. She and Slipper seemed welded together as they edged up until Slipper's head was level with the lead horse's flanks.

'It's going to be a photo finish!' yelled the commentator. 'Slipper's gaining on Rags to Riches.'

The finishing post was close now. With a final burst of speed, Slipper shot past her opponent and into the lead. Turf flew as she thundered past the post, and an almighty roar broke from the crowd. Slipper slowed to a trot and then a walk and Rose stood up from the saddle, acknowledging the applause with a flourish of her whip. De Silva was glad that she hadn't used it in the race.

Jane put a hand to her throat. 'Goodness, what an exciting race. I feel exhausted just from watching it.'

David Hebden laughed. 'I do too. I think I'll stick to cricket. The leisurely pace is more in tune with my temperament.'

Emerald squeezed his arm. 'Very sensible, dear. And less likelihood of injuring oneself. I'm sure the Applebys will be as relieved that Rose came through unscathed as they must be happy that she won. Before we collect our winnings, shall we go over to the unsaddling enclosure? If there's a chance, I'd like to congratulate her.'

'Very well.' He turned to the de Silvas. 'Will you come too?'

'That would be lovely,' said Jane. 'Although I expect a lot of people will want to congratulate her and we wouldn't like to intrude.'

When they reached the unsaddling enclosure, Jane proved to be right, so she and de Silva held back and let the Hebdens go in alone. De Silva observed that the same group of young men were already there, forming an animated group around Rose who had dismounted and was laughing and talking with them. She had removed her jockey's cap and apart from looking a little flushed, seemed remarkably composed. She still held Slipper's reins and was stroking her neck as she talked. Foam flecked the mare's lips and, darkened by sweat, her coat steamed.

A young man dressed in the clothes of a servant stood a little way off, watching the scene. There was something not quite right about him, thought de Silva. He looked awkward and anxious but there was more to it than that. Rose broke off her conversation and her gaze ranged over the people around her, stopping when it reached the young man. She beckoned to him and hesitantly, he came to join her and Slipper. She put her hand on his shoulder, squeezed it, and said something to him. If he was a servant, de Silva was a little surprised to see her behaving towards him in such a familiar way. He smiled bashfully and visibly relaxed then took the reins from her and started to lead Slipper away.

The Hebdens returned and they all went to collect their winnings then watched the next two races until it was time for the main race of the afternoon, the Hill Country Cup. The favourite was number six, Garnet, owned by Grace and Dickie de Jong. De Silva knew that they were one of the wealthiest tea planting families in the area who also owned large rubber plantations in the low country down by Kandy.

After studying the odds, he and Jane decided not to have a bet. The bookies were obviously very sure that Garnet would win, but just for fun the Hebdens wanted to put a small bet on one of the other horses, so they all went back to the paddock to take a look at them. Archie and Florence were already there, part of the group around Garnet.

Emerald giggled. 'Florence has surpassed herself this year,' she whispered to Jane. 'What a wonderful hat.'

It was indeed a remarkable hat, thought de Silva. With a brim that slanted at a sharp angle to Florence's face, it was made of some silky, strawberry-coloured material and crowned with a decoration in the shape of a horseshoe. The colour matched Florence's dress, her low-heeled court shoes, and her handbag. To de Silva the comparison with a giant fruit was irresistible.

Florence and Archie left the paddock, and the horses began to head for the start. Florence saw the Hebdens and the de Silvas, and she and Archie came over to greet them.

'Splendid afternoon, eh,' said Archie. 'I'm very glad that the ladies' race was such a success. Always nice to make a good start. Who knows? The Jockey Club may see fit to introduce a few more.'

'I hope so,' said Jane.

'Are you having a bet on this race?'

'As we won on Slipper, we've decided to rest on our laurels, and the odds for Garnet are so short.'

Archie nodded. 'Yes, Garnet does seem certain to win. Of course, he's one of the most valuable horses in Ceylon. Belongs to the de Jongs, who we've just been talking to. What about you, Hebden?'

'Emerald and I plan to have a modest bet on one of the other horses.'

'Why not, you never know with racing. You could do worse than Bright Star, another from the de Jong stable. Dickie de Jong was telling us that he's been coming along well this year. Not up to the same standard as Garnet, of course, but promising. He's won a few minor races and the de Jongs' trainer thought it was time to be more ambitious.'

Hebden turned to Emerald. 'What do you think, my love?'

'It sounds like a tip straight from the horse's mouth.'

'Right, I'll go and put our money on. Shall I see you back at the entrance to the grandstand as before?'

'That's a good idea.'

Archie and Florence joined Emerald and the de Silvas on the way to the grandstand, Archie walking in front chatting with Emerald and Jane, and de Silva in the rear with Florence who regaled him with her opinion of the de Jongs as they went.

'What was Florence telling you about the de Jongs?' asked Jane when the Clutterbucks had left them to go up to their box.

'Oh, I wasn't listening all that closely. It's often easiest to let the conversation flow over you when Florence is doing the talking.'

Jane smiled. 'I know what you mean.'

'I think she said something about Dickie being a charming man with a great sense of humour, but his wife Grace being rather aloof.'

'Perhaps she's just quiet unless she knows someone well.'

'She's always very elegantly dressed,' remarked Emerald. She lowered her voice. 'According to some people, as well as being charming, Dickie de Jong is a bit of a rogue. He splashes money around, but most of it comes from Grace's side of the family. And there are rumours he's sometimes too friendly with other women, if you know what I mean.'

'Oh dear.'

They slowed as they reached the grandstand to find a short queue of people waiting to get in.

Emerald glanced sideways. 'That's the de Jongs' son Eddie over there, talking to Rose Appleby.'

De Silva recognised the tall, fair-haired young man from the group around Rose after the ladies' race. He and Rose were talking very animatedly. Rose had changed into a yellow dress and looked even prettier than she had done in her riding kit.

'I've heard Eddie and his father don't always see eye to eye,' whispered Emerald. 'But his mother adores him despite the fact that he hasn't settled to anything and only seems interested in having fun and spending money. I believe he and Rose have been good friends since they were children, but it might be unfortunate if their friendship develops into something more. The Applebys like him but they don't think he's suitable husband material. Rose is independent minded, but she loves her parents. I think going against their wishes would make her very sad.'

As Emerald talked, de Silva watched Rose and Eddie. Now Eddie seemed to be telling her some long story and she was laughing. They certainly looked very relaxed together.

David Hebden returned, and they all took their places in the stand to watch the horses entered in the Hill Country Cup trot up the course to the starting line. Once there, they milled about waiting for the starter's gun. The field was much larger than it had been for the ladies' race. De Silva counted twenty horses.

The starting gun cracked, and the horses set off. Garnet, his chestnut coat gleaming in the sunshine, was amongst the leaders. His jockey didn't follow Rose's technique of holding him back until later on in the race, thought de Silva. Jane borrowed David Hebden's binoculars and studied the horses through them. 'Your horse Bright Star is doing quite well,' she said. 'Perhaps it will come second.'

'The de Jongs are sure to be thrilled if they take first and second place,' said Emerald.

The commentator's voice crackled over the loudspeaker system. 'Coming through on the outside, it's Bright Star. As they go into the home strait, he's moving up fast.'

Emerald clutched her husband's arm. 'Oh my goodness, David, isn't this exciting!'

As the horses covered the last few hundred yards to the finishing post, Bright Star gained more speed, passing his stable mate whose jockey was making liberal use of his whip to very little effect. To a roar of amazement, Bright Star streaked into first place and past the post.

A cheer rose from the crowd. 'It's Bright Star!' shouted the commentator. 'Bright Star wins the Hill Country Cup! Garnet, the favourite's, nowhere.'

'Gracious, that was unexpected,' said Jane.

David Hebden grinned. 'I think we ought to celebrate. The drinks are on us.'

'I don't expect Garnet's jockey will be happy that they only came fifth,' said Emerald.

'It goes to show that anything can happen in a race. Perhaps he was too confident of success. Still the de Jongs have won the cup, and if today's anything to go by, Bright Star has a bright future.'

The main bar in the grandstand enclosure was already busy, so they found a quieter one where Hebden ordered drinks: lemonade for de Silva and the ladies and a beer for himself. Beer was a taste that de Silva had never acquired. When Hebden had finished his, he stood up. 'I'd better go and collect our winnings, Emerald. Would you rather stay here?'

Emerald fanned herself. 'I think I will. It's so nice and cool.'

'I'll keep you company,' said Jane. She turned to de Silva. 'But there's no need to stay if you'd rather go with David and stretch your legs. We'll be perfectly fine.'

De Silva got to his feet. 'If you're sure about that, a walk would be pleasant.' Since he didn't usually bet at the races, he was curious to have another look around the area where the bookies were camped out. Partly, he had a professional interest, for one of his jobs as Chief Inspector of Police for Nuala was to make sure that gambling was properly regulated.

They found the bookie who had taken the Hebdens' bet and joined the queue of other people waiting to collect their winnings. De Silva noted that most of the bookies had a fairly long queue, as this one did. 'Not a good outcome for them,' remarked Hebden. 'Still, I'm sure they win out overall.'

'I expect you're right,' said de Silva absently. He was giving half an ear to the conversation of the two men in front of them.

'Strange result,' the taller one was saying to his companion. 'Garnet should have won that by a mile.'

The other man tapped a finger against his nose. 'Maybe someone had other plans.'

'Where did you hear that?'

'Oh, nowhere in particular, but we all know how rumours spread.' The taller man laughed. 'Sometimes they're even true.'

Hebden raised an eyebrow and the man glanced at him, probably noticing that someone was listening. He turned away from them before he continued speaking, this time in a quieter voice.

'If it comes to the de Jongs' ears that that kind of talk's going around, they won't be happy,' said Hebden after he'd pocketed his winnings and they were strolling through the crowd. 'Still there's probably nothing in it.'

They had just stopped to watch a small team of acrobats who were performing a show when they saw Rose's father, George Appleby. Hebden waved and he came over to speak to them.

'Lost your family?' asked Hebden jovially.

'They're about somewhere. As you may imagine, after Rose's win they're enjoying a lot of attention. I'm afraid, however, that my afternoon has turned out to be less pleasurable.'

'What do you mean?'

'There's a problem with the result of the main race.'

De Silva knew that as well as being the local veterinary

surgeon, George Appleby was the government veterinary adviser for the area. 'Are you involved?' he asked.

'So far, I've only been asked to take blood and saliva samples from Garnet and Bright Star for testing. I don't know whether the stewards will require me to do anything after that.'

'Testing? Do you mean the horses may have been drugged?' asked Hebden.

'It's possible. The result's unexpected enough to raise suspicion. If someone wanted to make sure that a horse put in a poor performance, the easiest way to do it would be to give it a bucket of water shortly before its race, but of course that's unlikely here. There would be far too many people about by then.'

'So, what are you looking for?'

'There are various drugs that unscrupulous owners are known to have experimented with. For example, morphine will slow racehorses down, whilst drugs based on caffeine produce the opposite effect. To be honest, the available tests for detecting drugs aren't foolproof, but they're the best we have to offer, and I expect the Jockey Club stewards will act on the results. But it's rotten luck for the de Jongs. Even if the tests come back negative, a cloud's likely to hang over their reputation. Hard on them if they're blameless. After all, even the best of horses can have a bad day and a novice does occasionally surprise everyone.'

'Are you off to take the samples now?' asked Hebden.

'Yes. Henry Fortescue, the chairman of the Jockey Club, and the other stewards are waiting for me. It might be a good idea if you came along. They can hardly object to a couple of reliable witnesses. Fortescue seems pretty confident no trace of drugs will be found and that will be the end of the matter. I hope he's right, but in case anyone asks questions, it would be handy to have you to vouch for it that everything was done in the proper manner.'

* * *

At the stables they found Henry Fortescue with four other men. He looked to be about the same age as Archie Clutterbuck and similarly heavily built. He glanced up as they approached.

'Ah, Appleby.' He nodded to de Silva and Hebden. 'Brought the cavalry with you, I see.'

'I asked Inspector de Silva and Doctor Hebden to accompany me as witnesses to the samples for testing being taken.'

'Good thinking,' rumbled Fortescue. De Silva was relieved that he raised no objection.

Hebden already knew some of the men present, but they were all strangers to de Silva. Brief introductions followed. Rupert Wilde, the deputy chairman, looked to be in his mid-thirties. Handsome with dark hair and a powerful physique, he exuded confidence. De Silva guessed that most women would find him attractive. The club secretary, Edmund Fallowfield, who appeared to be a few years older than Wilde, seemed less self-assured. He was as tall as Wilde but by no means as good-looking.

Next came Peter Findley, the clerk of the course, and the stables' manager, Pat Masham, both older men. Findley was slight, with a pale freckled complexion and sandy hair that was thinning on top. In contrast Pat Masham was built like a prize fighter. His leathery skin was deeply tanned, and his dark eyes looked as if they didn't miss much.

'I assume this needn't take long,' said Fortescue when the introductions were complete. 'My wife and I have important guests with us. I don't want to neglect them any longer than absolutely necessary. It's in the nature of racing for there to be upsets, y'know. I find it hard to believe that the de Jongs have been party to anything that infringes the rules, but best to be sure everything's above board. We need to be able to quash any rumours that may be flying around.' He turned to Pat Masham. 'May as well get on with it. Give Appleby a hand, would you?'

Together George Appleby and Masham went into Garnet's box. The big thoroughbred tossed his head and rolled his eyes and Masham had to take a firm grip on his headcollar to bring him under control. Appleby found a vein and quickly took the sample then both men made a swift exit from the box and Masham shut the lower half of the door firmly.

'Best to give him a bit of time to settle,' said Appleby. 'I've no wish to be crushed against a wall and I don't expect Masham has either.'

'To be sure I don't,' said Masham. His accent suggested to de Silva that he was Irish.

When Garnet was calmer, they went back into the box. This time, with Masham quietly soothing him and stroking his neck, Garnet submitted to a sample of saliva being taken. Dealing with Bright Star proved to be less of a challenge and after a few minutes, the task of taking samples was over.

The young man who had led Rose Appleby's mare out of the unsaddling enclosure for her hovered close by. Pat Masham called him over. De Silva noticed that once more he seemed anxious and ill at ease.

'Shall… shall I…' His next words were lost in confusion.

Masham smiled at him. 'Slowly, lad.'

The young man took a deep breath then spoke again. 'Shall I water the horses and rub them down, sahib?' The words still came out clumsily but this time they were comprehensible. He moved closer to Garnet and all at once, the big thoroughbred seemed a different animal, the look in his eyes soft and his manner calm whereas only a few moments ago he had radiated hostility.

'Yes,' said Masham, 'but first find the de Jongs' grooms.

They should be about somewhere. The horses are to stay here overnight and be ridden home in the morning.'

'Who is that lad?' asked de Silva as the young man hurried away.

'His name's Sunil. He works at the livery stables and does extra jobs for me when we have a meeting on. He's a magician with horses but—' Masham shrugged. 'As you can see for yourself, he's not quite right in the head. Willing and a very hard worker but he's no more idea of life than a baby. All the staff up here know to keep an eye out for him, but anyone ill-intentioned could wrap him around their little finger as easy as a tot of whisky slips down at the end of the day, and no mistake.'

Edmund Fallowfield, who stood next to Rupert Wilde and had said very little up to that point, unexpectedly gave his neighbour a sly look. 'Not a fellow to be trusted with one's darkest secrets, eh?'

'What do you mean by that?' asked Wilde in a sharp tone.

Fallowfield coloured slightly and gave an uncomfortable laugh. 'Only a joke.'

For a brief moment, there was an awkward pause then Masham spoke again. 'If there's nothing more to be done, I'll be leaving you.'

'Certainly,' said Fortescue. 'I expect you've plenty to be getting on with. I'm hoping to watch the last race myself, but I suppose I'd better have a word with Dickie de Jong first. I managed to convince him that it would be improper for him to be present when the samples were taken, but I expect he'll want to know it's been done. I've already spoken with Archie Clutterbuck, so I'll give him an update. Thank you for your help, Appleby. How soon do you think you'll be able to get the results of the tests to us? I'd like to have this unpleasant business over as quickly as possible.'

'Hopefully by the day after tomorrow at the latest. I'll tell the lab it's urgent.'

'Good. Naturally, we have to hold off presenting the Cup until the matter's resolved, which isn't a desirable situation. De Jong's furious of course. Threatening all sorts of things.' He shrugged. 'Despite the fact I've done my best to reassure him that this is just a case of observing protocol.'

'I can well believe that de Jong's kicking up a stink,' muttered George Appleby as he and de Silva walked away. 'He isn't a man to take a setback lying down.'

'Do you think he's innocent?'

'I hope so. It's a bad day for Nuala racing if he's not. All the same, I'm glad Henry Fortescue didn't try to apply any pressure on me to bury this. Luckily, he plays with a straight bat.'

How the British loved their cricketing metaphors, thought de Silva. 'What do you think was going on between Wilde and that fellow Fallowfield?' he asked.

'I couldn't say for sure. Wilde has quite a reputation with the ladies, perhaps that was what Fallowfield was alluding to. But I'm surprised he made the remark. My impression of him from our few previous meetings has been that he's a bit of a dull dog. Not Wilde's type at all. If he was trying to be chummy and josh Wilde, it obviously fell flat.'

* * *

'You were gone a long time,' said Emerald when Hebden and de Silva returned. George Appleby had already parted company with them to re-join his family.

Hebden lowered his voice. 'It isn't for anyone else's ears, but we've been with George Appleby and the stewards. Appleby took samples of blood and saliva from Garnet and Bright Star.'

'Does that mean the stewards think there's something in the rumours going around?' asked Emerald.

'You've heard people talking, have you?'

'Yes.'

'Henry Fortescue says he finds it hard to believe there's been wrongdoing, but he felt compelled to act.'

Emerald frowned. 'From what one hears the de Jongs are highly respected and have had plenty of success with their horses. Wouldn't it be foolish of them to try to cheat? All the same, it was odd. Garnet was hotly tipped to win and then didn't, and the de Jongs' other horse won and that was very unexpected.'

'So the horse with the short odds lost and the one with long odds won,' said Jane thoughtfully. 'Even if the de Jongs had backed both of them, they probably won more money than they lost and they would still receive the prize money and the Cup.'

'Exactly,' said Hebden.

'But I agree with Emerald. If the de Jongs are highly respected and have plenty of winners, wouldn't it be foolish of them to risk doing something underhand?'

De Silva shrugged. 'Maybe rich people think they can never be rich enough.'

'What will happen now, David?' asked Emerald.

'Appleby's going to have the samples checked as soon as possible and it will be taken from there.' He glanced around him. 'As I'm sure you'll agree, it's best we keep all of this under our hats.'

CHAPTER 2

That evening, as was their custom, Florence and Archie
threw a party at the Residence to mark the close of the race
meeting. It was a pity, thought de Silva, that this year the
day's events were likely to cast a shadow over the festivities.

It was dark by the time the party started and when he
and Jane arrived, the Residence's driveway was illuminated
by flaming torches. More torches had been placed in the
flowerbeds under the big white house's windows, bathing
the lower part of the façade in a warm glow. De Silva and
Jane joined the crowd of guests mounting the stairs of the
columned entrance portico. The reception hall beyond it
was adorned with splendid flower arrangements that gave
off delightful scents.

Florence and Archie's evening parties were usually
formal occasions, and this one was no exception. The ladies
wore long dresses and their best jewellery – Jane had
chosen a dark blue dress and added her favourite sapphire
necklace. Like most of the local men, de Silva sported
loose trousers and a white tunic. The tunic was adorned
with gold buttons, but some of the tunics being worn were
made entirely of gold silk, providing an exotic contrast to
the smart but severe black and white of the British men's
evening attire.

After guests had been greeted by Florence and Archie
in the receiving line, a waiter holding a silver tray offered

champagne and a variety of fruit juices; de Silva and Jane accepted glasses of mango juice. More waiters offered silver trays of canapés. De Silva took a tiny round of puff pastry filled with a yellow mixture. 'What do you think this is?' he asked Jane as the waiter moved on.

'A vol-au-vent. It means windblown in French because they're so light. Florence was very keen to serve them this evening. Apparently, she and Archie had them at one of the Petries' soirées at Government House in Kandy.'

'That's certainly a good recommendation.' He popped the pastry into his mouth. The filling tasted like mashed egg with salad cream. 'Not bad,' he said once he'd swallowed it. 'Not bad at all.'

'When I was doing the church flowers with Florence last Sunday, she told me she'd been hoping to have some of the vol-au-vents filled with salmon, but tinned salmon is hard to come by at the moment. Still, we mustn't grumble when there's food rationing in England because of the war.'

De Silva was aware that numerous foodstuffs were in short supply in England, amongst them tea, margarine, jam, sugar, and marmalade, and people had to make do with very limited amounts. It had recently been reported in the newspaper that clothes were also being rationed. People were urged to make their winter coats out of spare blankets.

He and Jane began to circulate, chatting to friends and acquaintances until he found himself separated from Jane and saw Archie approaching.

'Having a good time, de Silva?'

De Silva nodded. 'It's an excellent party, sir.'

'I can't take any credit. Florence sees to all this kind of thing. Seems to make a very good job of it too. I don't know what I'd do without her. As you know, fishing and golf are more my line.' Archie lowered his voice. 'Tell me, what do you think about the problem at the racecourse today?'

'I'm no expert in these matters.'

'Very diplomatic of you. Between ourselves, I can't help feeling it's a pity that we have to hold the party this evening. Dashed awkward in the circumstances. Naturally, Dickie and Grace de Jong were invited. That's them over there talking to my wife.' He nodded in the direction of a middle-aged man who had once, no doubt, been strikingly handsome but was running to seed. The lady with him was very elegantly dressed and had a lovely face but her expression was strained. Like her husband, she had a pale complexion, although her hair was almost black. The couple's name indicated to de Silva that the de Jongs were of Dutch burgher stock, a group of people who still enjoyed high social standing in Ceylon society.

'Now that the presentation of the Cup has been held up until the result of the inquiry comes in,' Archie went on, 'people can hardly fail to know there's a cloud hanging over them, but it would have been very awkward to withdraw their invitation. Innocent until proved guilty and all that. I wondered if they'd make an excuse not to turn up, although from what I know of him, Dickie de Jong isn't a man to shy away from trouble. I suppose if he's done nothing wrong, that's to his credit, but their presence is causing a lot of comment.'

Archie took a sip of his champagne and stifled a sneeze. 'This damnable stuff gets up my nose, but Florence has banned me from having a whisky this evening. Anyway, back to the de Jongs. The reason I didn't join you when Appleby carried out those tests was that we had important guests in our box. I didn't want to make heavy weather of the situation by going off and leaving them, but Fortescue's filled me in on what went on. He's pretty bullish about it being a storm in a teacup, leaving us free to award the prize to the de Jongs. I hope he's right.'

'Indeed, sir. What will happen if the tests are positive?'

'If that's the case, we have to find the culprit. If the de

Jongs' jockeys or one of their grooms were responsible, they'd be banned from racing for the foreseeable future.'

'What about the de Jongs themselves?'

'If the Jockey Club concludes that they put any of their people up to it, they'll receive a fine and a ban for the rest of the season.'

But they wouldn't be in danger of losing their livelihood as a jockey or a groom would, thought de Silva.

'I can see what you're thinking,' said Archie. 'But the damage to the de Jongs' reputation would be a severe punishment for them. They've always been stalwarts of the racing community over here. Even if the inquiry exonerates them, things might still be unpleasant for them. When mud's been thrown, it often sticks. Wealthy people like the de Jongs tend to attract enemies, often motivated by jealousy. Such people might be happy to throw doubt on the result of the tests. As a lot of people in the racing fraternity will be aware, they aren't entirely reliable.'

'George Appleby mentioned that.'

Archie cast a glance to his left to where an elderly couple was bearing down on them. 'Duty calls,' he muttered. 'Keep your ears open and eyes peeled, will you? If there's anything you think I might want to know, come to see me in the morning.'

Leaving Archie to talk to the elderly couple, de Silva went to find Jane. As he weaved his way through the crowd, he caught sight of the de Jongs again. Their son Eddie was with them, and they were talking to Rose Appleby and Rupert Wilde. The conversation between Rose and the three men seemed lively but Grace looked to be miles away. De Silva wondered whether she was more sensitive to unpleasantness than her husband. He certainly looked as if he didn't have a care in the world.

It was traditional for there to be dancing at the party, and when de Silva found Jane, they watched the dance band make their preparations. The Residence's grand piano had been moved out from its usual place in one corner of the ballroom and a drum kit was already set up. The drummer and the pianist took their places and were joined by a saxophone player, a trombonist, and a double bass player, all of them dressed in white tie and tails. Finally, the band's singer arrived. She wore a flame-red dress with a chiffon skirt and a sequinned bodice; her platinum blonde hair shone in the light of the chandeliers. The final member of the ensemble to arrive was the conductor. Like the other men, he wore white tie and tails. His dark hair, sharply parted in the centre, gleamed with brilliantine. He raised his baton and paused a moment then began to beat time. Music cut through the laughter and talk.

'This number's rather fast,' said de Silva. 'Shall we sit it out? Perhaps the band will play something more suited to my old legs later on.'

Jane raised an eyebrow. 'As long as you promise not to make that excuse all evening.'

'I promise.'

Retreating to the nearby wall, they sat down on two of the spindly gilt and velvet chairs that were arranged along it. De Silva sighed. He knew this type of seat was popular with the British on formal occasions, but why did they choose one that felt so precarious and uncomfortable?

They had watched the dancers for five minutes before he noticed the Hebdens standing not far away with Rose Appleby. Emerald beckoned to them, and they got up and went over to say hello.

'I think you were still a little girl when we last met,' said Jane to Rose. 'I hear you're working as a reporter on the *Nuala Times* now. How exciting.'

Rose made a face. 'Not quite as exciting as I'd hoped. I've not been given much to do yet, apart from reporting on charity sales and church events.'

'That kind of thing is important to the community,' said Jane mildly.

'Of course.' Rose gave her an apologetic smile. 'And I appreciate it's a good thing if life in Nuala is peaceful.'

David Hebden chuckled. 'I wouldn't be too sure about that. I hear things can get pretty warm in the meetings of these organising committees.'

Emerald gave him a look of mock reproof. 'What nonsense!'

'Still, riding must provide you with plenty of excitement, Rose,' Jane went on. 'Shanti and I were very impressed with your performance today. How thrilling that you won, especially as it's the first time a ladies' race has been run in Nuala.'

'You're very kind, and yes, I am thrilled, but I fear it might have been beginner's luck.'

'Surely not.'

'I'm absolutely certain it wasn't,' said a deep, rich voice. De Silva turned to see that Dickie de Jong had joined them. He appeared to be in high spirits despite the situation he was in. His son Eddie was still with him but there was no sign of Grace. Dickie raised his glass of champagne. 'To Rose! May this be the first of many victories.'

Rose laughed. 'Thank you.'

Dickie drained his glass and glanced over his shoulder. 'Never a waiter around when you need one,' he muttered.

Rose introduced them all and they chatted until the band struck up a quickstep and Eddie asked Rose to dance.

'Are you a dancer, Mrs de Silva?' asked Dickie as the two young people took to the floor.

Jane smiled. 'I enjoy dancing, but my husband isn't always keen.'

'I only ask that we wait for a slow dance,' said de Silva apologetically.

Dickie de Jong held out a hand. 'Then if he has no objection, may I have this one?'

'With pleasure.'

'I don't know what my son learned from that very expensive education I paid for, but it wasn't dancing, that's for sure,' remarked Dickie as he steered Jane somewhat unsteadily through the crowd of dancers. They were passing close enough to Eddie and Rose for his words to be heard but although Eddie shot his father a baleful look, Dickie wasn't to be deterred. 'Eton and Oxford; impossible to buy a better education anywhere in the world,' he said loudly. 'Not that he's made good use of it.'

The dance came to an end. Followed by Rose and Eddie, who still looked annoyed, Dickie and Jane returned to de Silva and the Hebdens. Dickie turned abruptly to David Hebden. 'Do you have children, Doctor Hebden?'

'A little girl. Her name's Olivia.'

'A pretty name. You're a lucky man. Daughters are far less trouble than sons.' His voice had begun to sound slurred. De Silva decided that he must have drunk more of the Clutterbucks' champagne than was good for him.

'I'm sure all children are a joy,' said Jane quickly, trying to head off the awkward atmosphere that threatened to descend on the group.

'Ah, there you are!' said a male voice.

De Silva imagined he wasn't the only one who felt relieved when, turning, he saw a tall young man with curly brown hair and a pleasant smile coming towards them.

'I've been looking for you all over, Eddie. Good evening, Mr de Jong. Quite a crush here, isn't it?'

With a visible effort at recovering his good humour, Eddie introduced the young man as his friend Toby Heatherington.

'Is this your first visit to Ceylon, Mr Heatherington?' asked Jane.

'Oh, please call me Toby. Indeed it is, although I grew up in India. My father was in the colonial service in Bombay.

I've made it my home too and I enjoy the bustle of the big city, but Nuala and the hill country make a delightful contrast. I wish I'd become acquainted with the area long ago. When Eddie and I were at school together in England, he often told me stories of his life growing up here, but nothing prepared me for the beauty of it all.'

'I'm glad you approve. Will you be staying in Nuala long?'

'Unfortunately not. I'll be sorry to leave, but I have to be back in Bombay by the end of the month.'

'Are you in the colonial service like your father?'

'No, nothing as important.' Toby turned to Rose. 'Congratulations on your splendid performance this afternoon.'

'Thank you, everyone has been so kind, but I was just saying that I fear I may have benefitted from beginner's luck.'

'From what I saw, I find it hard to believe luck had anything to do with it. Anyway, I'm very grateful to you. I won a good deal of money. Actually, it *was* a bit of luck I made it in time to watch the race. I had to go out of town and the trip took longer than I'd anticipated, then I had to find my way up to the course. I must say, it's a charming spot with splendid views.'

'I thought you might have been before.'

'No, it was my first time. A while ago Eddie mentioned something about driving up to see the sun go down as it's a great spot for that, but there hasn't been time. In any case, your race provided a far more exciting introduction.'

Eddie, his equilibrium apparently fully restored, gave his friend a punch in the ribs. 'That's enough turning on the charm, old chap.' The band had begun to play once more, and he held out his hand to Rose. 'Dance with me again?'

Rose nodded and took his hand.

'Shall we dance too, David?' asked Emerald.

'If you'd like to.'

The Hebdens followed Eddie and Rose onto the dance-floor leaving Jane and de Silva with Dickie de Jong and Toby. They chatted for a while then out of the corner of his eye, de Silva noticed Grace de Jong coming into the ballroom through one of the French windows that led to the terrace. She walked over to them and, swaying a little, her husband wrapped his arm around her waist. De Silva saw her tense. Perhaps she thought as he did that Dickie had drunk too much champagne.

'Shall we dance, my love?' Dickie asked.

'No, I'm tired. I'd rather go home.'

Her husband pulled a face and his grip tightened. 'But we'll miss all the fun. Can't I have one dance with my darling wife?'

A furrow appeared between Grace's elegantly arched eyebrows. 'I've told you. I'm tired and I don't want to dance.'

'Why don't I drive Mrs de Jong home?' asked Toby.

Grace turned to him and smiled wanly. 'That would be very kind. But I hope you'll come back after that. I wouldn't want to spoil your evening.'

'Oh no,' said Dickie in a sour voice. 'I'm sure we wouldn't want anyone's evening spoiled.'

Grace threw him a crushing look and took Toby's arm. 'It was a pleasure to meet you and your husband, Mrs de Silva. I hope to see you again.'

They walked away and de Silva saw them stop for a few moments to speak to Archie. After they'd gone, he came over.

'I'm sorry your wife feels out of sorts, de Jong. I sympathise with her. Crowded places aren't really my cup of tea either.'

Dickie glowered. 'It seems it's always too crowded when I'm around.'

There was an awkward silence, broken by Archie. 'Well,

never mind. I think it's time I got some air m'self. If these good people will excuse us, why not join me?'

Dickie's expression resembled that of an obstinate bulldog, but he nodded.

'So what do you make of that?' asked Jane as the two men headed for the terrace. 'Dickie de Jong does seem an odd man, and he's clearly had too much to drink this evening. When we were dancing, he made some very unkind remarks about his son that I'm sure Eddie heard, and I suspect his father meant him to, and did the same when he asked David about his family. So he's happy to criticise Eddie before people who are virtually strangers but behaves badly himself. And he and his wife certainly don't seem to be a happy couple.'

'No, they don't. It was just as well that young man Toby was there to play peacemaker before the situation turned nasty.'

'I found him very pleasant. I wonder why he was so uncommunicative about his work.'

De Silva shrugged. 'I've no idea.'

'I suppose he might be involved in the war effort. If that's the case, it might be something very important that he has to keep quiet about.'

'You have a romantic imagination, my love,' said de Silva with a smile. 'There's no conscription in this part of the world so he may have nothing at all to do with the war, any more than his friend Eddie does.'

'Eddie and Rose Appleby seem keen on each other.'

De Silva rolled his eyes and Jane giggled. 'What's that for?'

'You and your matchmaking.'

'It's nothing of the sort.'

'Well, let's hope for her sake that he hasn't inherited his father's less desirable characteristics.'

'Yes, let's. Poor Grace de Jong,' Jane added sadly. 'I hope

she doesn't have to put up with too much bad behaviour from her husband.'

'At least the situation was saved this evening. You might say all is well that ends well.' He cupped a hand to his ear. 'Now the band's playing something I will venture to dance to. Shall we?'

CHAPTER 3

De Silva and Jane were eating breakfast the following morning when the telephone rang in the hall.

'Were you expecting a call?' he asked.

'No, were you?'

De Silva shook his head and sighed. An unanticipated telephone call early on a Sunday morning was likely to mean unwelcome news. Quickly, he scooped the last morsel of his soft-boiled egg into his mouth, but the ringing stopped and none of the servants came to call him. *Probably a wrong number*, he thought with relief. A few minutes later, however, there was a knock at the door and their servant Jayasena came in.

'I'm sorry to disturb you, sahib.'

De Silva was concerned to see that Jayasena, who was usually so calm, looked very upset.

'There's no need to apologise. Is there a problem?'

'If you do not need me this morning, I'd like to go up to the racecourse.'

'The racecourse? Why do you want to go there?'

'It is my nephew, Sunil.' Jayasena swallowed hard and de Silva saw there were tears in his eyes. 'He has been found dead, sahib.'

Sunil: de Silva's ears pricked up. Wasn't that the name of the young man who had asked if he should water and rub down the de Jongs' horses after George Appleby had tested them? He'd also noticed him leading Rose Appleby's mare into the winners' enclosure after Rose had won her race.

Jane stood up and went to put a hand on Jayasena's shoulder. 'Oh, Jayasena, I'm so sorry. What happened?'

'Sahib Masham has just telephoned. He says it was an accident. That's all I know. I am needed to identify Sunil's body. Sahib Masham says it is—'

He stopped and took a moment to compose himself before continuing. 'A formality that must be observed. There will need to be arrangements made for the cremation too.' He shook his head sadly. 'It will be very hard for my sister to hear the news, and hard for me to tell it to her.'

De Silva stood up, mopping a smear of egg from his lips with his napkin. 'I'll drive you there.'

'There is no need, sahib. I will manage somehow.'

'Nonsense. I wouldn't dream of letting you go on your own.'

* * *

'Tell me about your nephew,' he said as the Morris rattled up the steep road to the racecourse.

'He was the son of my widowed sister. Her husband died not long after Sunil was born, and she has no other children. My sister was so happy when he got his job at the racecourse. All our family were glad too. Sunil had some difficulties, and Sahib Masham was very kind to him. He gave him jobs he could manage quite easily – mucking out stables and cleaning tack for the people who keep their horses at the livery yard. There is more work to do when race meetings are on, but Sahib Masham made sure Sunil did not have heavier duties than he was able to cope with. The sahib praised Sunil because he was so good with the horses.'

De Silva was sure now that Jayasena's nephew was the

young man that he'd seen at the races. 'It sounds as if it was a very satisfactory arrangement,' he remarked.

Jayasena nodded. 'Not everyone is as kind as Sahib Masham. Because my nephew was like a child in many ways and trusted people too much, my family has always worried that people would take advantage of him. My sister was very anxious when he didn't come home last night after he should have finished work. I tried to comfort her that he might have gone out to celebrate with some of the other stable lads.'

De Silva nodded. 'A reasonable assumption. There's always a lot going on in town after the Hill Country Cup meeting.'

'Yes, sahib. Much dancing and eating and drinking. Although I only saw Sunil drink arrack once and it made him sick. After that, I only saw him drink a little beer. I said to my sister it must have grown late and he had slept at the home of a friend.'

His voice cracked. 'I told her the only thing she had to fear was that he would oversleep and be late for work, but Sahib Masham would probably overlook that.' He dashed tears out of his eyes. 'If I had gone to look for him, perhaps I would have found him and brought him safely home.'

'You mustn't blame yourself,' de Silva said gently. 'We don't know exactly what happened yet. The accident might well have been unavoidable.'

They reached the livery yard and found Pat Masham in one of the barns with the Jockey Club secretary, Edmund Fallowfield, and David Hebden. The barn had a floor of beaten earth and looked to be used as a tack room. Bridles hung from hooks or large nails on the walls and there was a long table made of roughly planed wood that had numerous saddles on it. At one end of it there was an assortment of tins, stiff brushes, and cloths. De Silva smelled leather and the pleasant aroma of beeswax.

Visibly distressed, Masham came forward and patted Jayasena's arm. 'I'm very sorry, Jayasena. I know how fond of Sunil you were. It seems he fell from the ladder that goes up to the hayloft up there.' He indicated the loft and then a long ladder lying on the ground. 'That's the ladder there. It fell on top of him and smashed into the poor lad's face. That explains the blood on his shirt. We got the ladder off him and cleaned him up as best we could.'

'He was unlucky,' said Hebden. 'If he'd hit the ground any other way, he would probably have escaped with a few broken bones plus the cuts and bruises from the ladder, but I'm afraid he must have fallen headfirst. At least it would have been quick. His neck was probably already broken by the time the ladder landed on his face.'

De Silva looked at the young man who lay dead on the ground. 'I saw him yesterday at the races,' he said. 'He was in charge of Rose Appleby's horse after her race.' Best not to mention seeing him again when the de Jongs' horses were tested.

Jayasena nodded. 'My sister has worked for the Appleby family since Sunil was a baby. He and Miss Rose grew up together.'

'She'll be very upset,' said Masham. 'She told me once that Sunil was like a younger brother to her.'

De Silva went over to Sunil's body and knelt down, straw crackling beneath his weight. The young man's head lolled at an awkward angle to his body. His face was disfigured by cuts and bruises and his neck was swollen. There was a smell of arrack.

'He probably died instantly,' said Hebden. 'Or certainly very soon after he fell.'

'It would be a blessing if he didn't suffer any pain,' said Masham solemnly.

'What would you estimate to be the time of death, Hebden?' asked de Silva.

'Mid to late evening. His body was found by one of the other stable lads early this morning.'

'He came straight to find me,' said Pat Masham. 'I live up here. Understandably, he was very distressed. It was a while before I could make sense of what he was saying. When I understood, I came straight here and found poor Sunil.'

'What time was it by then?'

'Nearly seven o'clock. Luckily, I have a key to the office. I knew that Jayasena was Sunil's uncle and that he worked for you. I looked up your telephone number and called. I thought it would be best for Jayasena to tell the boy's mother once he'd formally identified the body. His death will be very distressing for her.'

De Silva hauled himself to his feet and went to examine the ladder.

'So, you believe he fell off this.' He took hold of the side struts and shook them. 'It seems steady enough.' As he peered up through the dim light that fell from a little window to one side of the hayloft, motes of chaff made his nose prickle.

'One of the rungs near the top is missing,' said Fallowfield, speaking for the first time. Unlike Masham, he wasn't showing any signs of distress and stood with his right hand in the pocket of his jacket in the casually authoritative pose de Silva had noticed in various portraits of British bigwigs that he'd seen. To be fair, however, he might hardly have known Sunil, and probably regarded safety at the stables as more Masham's responsibility than his. 'Broken away,' he went on, reaching down with his free hand to pick up a piece of wood. 'Here it is. Sunil may have managed to climb up to the hayloft without mishap. My guess is that it was on the way down that he lost his footing. He'd probably had a few drinks. I understand he wasn't used to drinking.'

'No alcohol's allowed at the stables on my watch,'

snapped Pat Masham. 'If he had a drink, he didn't get it here. And that ladder was in good condition. Everything here's properly maintained.'

The air crackled with antipathy, but Fallowfield merely shrugged. 'I can't think of any other explanation for why the accident happened, can you? And as far as safety's concerned, it never does any harm to take a fresh look at procedures, does it?'

Masham shot him an angry glance.

De Silva looked to find out where Jayasena had gone and saw him kneeling by Sunil's body, smoothing the dark hair from the young man's forehead.

'Perhaps he was planning to sleep up there,' said Hebden. 'But if you're right about his fall being on the way down, why was he trying to come down before morning?'

Fallowfield shrugged. 'Answering a call of nature?'

De Silva went over to Jayasena who raised a stricken face to his. 'Who would let him have arrack?' he asked bitterly.

'I don't know, Jayasena, but I'll do my best to find out and make them understand what a bad thing they did.' He looked at Sunil's lifeless body. Sadly, no amount of remorse on the part of anyone who had let him have strong drink would bring him back.

'I'll put the barn out of bounds until the body can be moved,' said Fallowfield. 'You'd better help with that, Masham.'

'Of course.' There was resentment in Masham's abrupt tone. He didn't meet Fallowfield's eye.

'I'd like to speak to the rest of the stable lads,' said de Silva.

Fallowfield nodded. 'Good idea. You can find out if they've anything to say about how the lad got in this state. Arrange that too, will you, Masham?'

Masham's expression was thunderous. 'They all knew Sunil needed to be treated with care.'

'That may be, but excitement runs high on Hill Country Cup day. Some of them may have overstepped the mark without meaning any harm. They won't be punished but they need to be aware of the error of their ways.'

Half an hour later, Sunil's body had been shrouded in a hastily found cloth and was on the way to town in one of the racecourse's jeeps with Pat Masham driving. Jayasena went with him. David Hebden had already gone home leaving de Silva with Fallowfield.

'Not a good start to the day,' Fallowfield remarked as they walked to the yard outside his office. 'May I offer you some tea before you go?'

De Silva thought of his interrupted breakfast, and the idea of learning more of Fallowfield. 'Thank you. That would be most welcome.'

Fallowfield led the way into an office furnished with a large desk, several straight-backed wooden chairs and numerous metal filing cabinets. A worn rug partially covered the floor, and thin curtains whose colour had long ago faded hung at the window.

'Not very luxurious, I'm afraid,' said Fallowfield. 'I've not been here long, and my predecessor left things in a bit of a mess, so I've had more to think about than my personal comfort.'

He went to a door at the far end of the room and called out. Soon, a skinny old man appeared in a loincloth that didn't look too clean.

'Bring us some tea,' said Fallowfield.

As the old man left the room, Fallowfield sat down behind his desk and motioned de Silva to take one of the other chairs.

'I didn't want to say anything with Sunil's uncle listening – he was clearly very fond of the boy – but I wouldn't be surprised if he drank more than the family knew. I didn't see much of him but when I did, I noticed that he tried very hard to keep up with his more able colleagues. Many of them are young. I wouldn't expect them to act as nurse-maids to the unfortunate lad.' He smiled sadly. 'What does the bible say? Am I my brother's keeper?'

De Silva waited for Fallowfield to go on.

'All I'm saying is that on such a big day, especially with Rose Appleby winning her race, the lad might have been even more desperate than usual to keep up. My guess is that he had too much to drink and was then afraid to go home, knowing he'd be in hot water. Somehow, he got himself back up here intending to sleep it off, ending as we've seen in this tragic accident.'

As de Silva digested this version of events, the tea arrived. It tasted better than he'd expected. They talked more as they drank it and de Silva learned that Fallowfield had come to Nuala six months ago after working for several years in Bombay.

'Way back, my family lived in India,' he said. 'My grand-parents came over from England in the 1870s. My grandfa-ther started up a successful business which my father took over after Grandfather died, but sadly Father died young. My mother sold up and returned to her family in England where I spent the remainder of my childhood, but I always wanted to return to this part of the world. Horses were my father's great love, and I inherited his passion. After a short spell in the army, I decided to try my luck in Bombay and look for work in the racing world.'

'I imagine that kind of work provides more excitement in Bombay than in our sleepy little town.'

'Don't do Nuala down. There may be fewer race meetings here, but they're of a high standard. Anyway, I'd reached an age when the prospect of a quieter life than that which the big city offers was increasingly attractive.'

'I felt much the same when I moved up from Colombo. My wife agreed and we've been very happy here.'

'You're a lucky man. I've never married. Couldn't seem to find the right girl.'

'Perhaps it is not too late.'

'Oh, I doubt that. One becomes set in one's ways.' Fallowfield smiled. 'A confirmed bachelor, that's me. Some of us are happiest in our own company.'

'You mentioned spending time in the army. Were you stationed in India?'

'No, Burma. And it was actually the military police. Our job was to keep an eye out for anything that might lead to an outbreak of civil disobedience. I'm afraid it wasn't always a pleasant task. At least in war you know who your enemy is. It's in so-called peace that things can get messy. Into the bargain, the heat in the jungle post where I was stationed made the weather down here seem temperate. I wasn't sorry when I handed in my baton. Of course, I expect there are times when you don't find your job easy.'

De Silva smiled. 'I doubt you'd find a policeman anywhere who would deny that.'

'But still you persevere.'

'My father was in the police force, so I suppose it runs in the blood. Anyway, I like the life in Nuala even when it presents challenges.'

'I'm glad to hear it.' Fallowfield drained his tea then looked at his watch. 'I'm not sure how much longer Pat Masham will be gone, and I don't want to make you take an extra trip. I'll tell you what, why don't I call the lads together now and you can ask your questions?'

'Thank you, that would be most helpful.'

* * *

'I spoke to all the people who worked with Sunil at the livery stable,' said de Silva. He had driven home to fill Jane in on the morning's events and they were sitting on the verandah with glasses of greenish-coloured juice in their hands, waiting for lunch to be served. De Silva would have preferred an Elephant ginger beer, but this concoction was something Jane had decided they should try. She'd been told by Florence Clutterbuck that it was good for the health, but even though the juice was mixed with jaggery and a few pinches of spice, to de Silva's mind, it needed to have a great many health benefits to make it worth drinking. At least Jane hadn't suggested it as a replacement for his evening whisky and soda.

'They were adamant that he didn't come into town with them to join in the festivities,' he continued. 'Apparently, he went along one year, and it was all too much for him – too much noise and too many crowds. He became quite frightened and never wanted to go again. When they left for town, he was with Rose Appleby's horse, Slipper. He was very close to Rose. He said he wanted to stay for a while and clean Slipper's tack for her. They assumed that when he'd finished, he'd go home.'

'But obviously he didn't. What puzzles me is why there was that smell of arrack you say you noticed around his body. Jayasena claimed Sunil never drank it again after it made him sick. Was there any evidence that he'd been sick before he died?'

'No, and I agree that's strange, but Edmund Fallowfield, the Jockey Club secretary who works up at the course, suggested that with the excitement of Rose's win, Sunil was likely to be even more desperate than usual to keep up with the other lads.'

'What did you make of Fallowfield?'

'He was abrupt at first, and there's clearly friction between him and Pat Masham who's in charge of the stables. Masham didn't at all like Fallowfield's insinuation that the ladder Sunil fell from might not have been kept in good condition and safety procedures weren't up to scratch.'

'Presumably, something like that would be Masham's responsibility?'

'I imagine so.'

Jane was silent for a few moments. De Silva swallowed a mouthful of his green juice, and Bella, who was curled up on his lap, stirred and sniffed the air before yawning and tucking her head back under her paws. She wasn't impressed by the juice's health benefits either, he thought. 'What's on your mind?' he asked Jane.

'That something about the story doesn't ring true. I don't think Jayasena would be wrong about his own nephew's drinking habits.'

'Are you suggesting this wasn't an accident? I agree we ought not to rule out anything at this stage, but it's hard to see why anyone would want to kill a harmless young man like Sunil.'

'I agree, but I think we ought to give it serious consideration.'

'According to the lads, there was no one but Sunil at the stables when they left.'

'Someone might have remained behind undetected.' Jane paused before continuing. 'It will be interesting to see how the inquiry into the result of the Hill Country Cup turns out.'

'Are you thinking it might be true that those two horses were doped, and Sunil saw something he wasn't meant to? Something that made it necessary for him to be silenced?'

Jane nodded. 'You read my mind.'

'Hmm. There are a lot of ifs and buts, but perhaps after lunch I ought to go back to the racecourse for a better look around.'

'That's a really good idea. Why don't I come with you?'

CHAPTER 4

After a hasty lunch, Jane and de Silva drove to the race-course. It seemed like a different place without the hustle and bustle of a race day. The fierce afternoon sun beat down on the track, leaching colour from the turf and reflecting sharply off the white rails that edged it. The area around the grandstand that had so recently swarmed with racegoers, entertainers, fortune tellers, and betting stalls looked dusty and forlorn.

Since there was no one around, they were saved from having to explain their visit, although if they had been challenged, de Silva had planned to say that he needed to refresh his memory of the scene of the accident for a report he was writing. It wasn't a complete lie. In the course of his duties, where there had been a fatal accident, he was bound to make a formal report.

As they made their way to the barn, a dainty grey mare put her head over the lower door of her box and regarded them mournfully. She twitched her head to dislodge the flies that gathered around her long-lashed eyes and whinnied. De Silva had never been particularly confident with horses, but her gentle demeanour encouraged him to stop and stroke her.

The occupant of the box a few doors further on was a different proposition – a black stallion with a white blaze that was a giant compared with the mare. The stallion gave them a baleful stare and tossed his head, knocking into the rim of the loose box's door and making it shake in its frame.

'I think we'll keep well clear of that one,' said de Silva.

'Perhaps it's just the heat making him irritable.'

'I wouldn't be too sure about that.'

Jane paused. 'He's very striking. I'm fairly certain he was one of the runners in the men's amateur jockeys' race yesterday.'

De Silva studied the stallion. 'I think you're right, and I recall that his jockey was Rupert Wilde.'

'Who's he?'

'One of the men I met with David Hebden and George Appleby on the day of the races. He's deputy chairman of the Jockey Club.' He remembered there had been something he hadn't liked about the man: an air of arrogant menace.

The heavy barn door creaked as he pushed it open; inside, the light was dim. The ladder had been removed from the place where Sunil's body had lain. De Silva frowned. 'I'm regretting I didn't give instructions for the scene to be left as it was found. I'd like a good look at that ladder.'

'If there really was foul play, you might have aroused the perpetrator's suspicions.' Jane glanced around the barn. 'The ladder's probably still here somewhere.'

After a short search, Jane found it lying on its side in a dark corner, 'Here it is!' she called. 'But we'll need to lift it out to where there's more light. It's far too dark here to examine it properly.'

De Silva went to join her. 'I can manage it on my own.'

'Don't be silly, it looks very heavy. I'll take this end and you take the other.'

'Any sign of the broken-off rung?'

'No. But that's not surprising, they'd have no reason to keep it.'

They carried the ladder out and put it down in the patch of sunshine that shone through the door into the barn. De

Silva had to admit he was a little out of breath by the time they had finished. 'You were right about it being heavy, and I'm afraid we'd better put it back where we found it after we've checked it.'

'Never mind.'

He knelt down in the straw and carefully began to go over the ladder. When he reached the broken rung, he ran the pad of his thumb over the remaining pieces of wood sticking out from the ladder's side struts. They were about the thickness of both of his thumbs put together.

'Watch out that you don't get a splinter,' said Jane.

'I'll be careful. Actually, what's left of the rung is surprisingly thick for it to have broken under Sunil's weight. In fact in general the wood looks to be in good condition.' De Silva brought his face closer to the ladder and squinted at the broken edges. 'I think the breakage isn't quite what it seems. I suspect that rung was partly cut through at each end, perhaps by a small axe, then broken off.'

He sat back on his heels and paused a moment. 'In other words, the damage was deliberate, and that puts a very different complexion on matters.'

*　*　*

'It's too much of a coincidence that Sunil's supposed accident happened on the same day as the Hill Country Cup,' said Jane as they drove back to Nuala. 'What do you think now about my theory that the poor boy saw something he wasn't supposed to?'

'You may have hit on something.'

'And what he saw would incriminate someone, the obvious crime being that they were doping either or both of Garnet and Bright Star.'

'If Dickie de Jong is behind this, I doubt he'd have done

the deed himself. He would be too easily recognised, but it might have been done by someone working for him.'

'Or an outsider who would be more easily able to conceal their identity and their connection to Dickie.'

'Hmm.' De Silva nodded as he slowed at the junction of the racecourse road and the main road back to town. There was something niggling in his brain that he couldn't quite remember.

A little further on, he noticed by the side of the road the carcass of a monitor lizard that must have been too slow getting out of the way of a passing car. At the Morris's approach, the four crows that had been pecking at it rose into the air in a flurry of offended squawks and black wings, and what he'd been trying to recall came to him. It was the remark that Edmund Fallowfield had made to Rupert Wilde. Fallowfield had said something about not entrusting one's darkest secrets to Sunil. The remark had fallen flat, obviously annoying Wilde, perhaps because he thought Fallowfield was referring to his reputation with the ladies and trying to make an overly familiar joke. But was there another reason why he was annoyed? Had the secretary unintentionally hit a raw nerve?

'Could it be that Wilde was involved in tampering with those horses?' mused Jane when he told her about the incident. 'It does seem rather unlikely that a member of the Jockey Club would risk doing such a thing.'

'I'm probably barking up the wrong tree.'

'No, you might not be. What would Wilde's motive be? The obvious one is money, of course. Would there be a way of finding out if he put a large bet on Bright Star?'

'It might be difficult. If he did, he wouldn't necessarily have used any of the Nuala bookies, but we can try them. I'll give Prasanna and Nadar the job of making general inquiries. It would be interesting to know if any notable bets were placed on Bright Star.'

'Another possibility is that he dislikes Dickie de Jong and wanted to do him a bad turn.'

'I'm not sure how we'd find out whether they get on or not, but it's also something to bear in mind.'

The Morris turned into the road that led to Sunnybank. 'I'd hoped for a bit of peace and quiet for a while,' said de Silva gloomily. 'It looks like we might not get it.'

CHAPTER 5

The following morning, one of the stable lads saddled Slipper for Rose then led the mare out to the mounting block in the yard. He held her steady as Rose climbed into the saddle and then handed her the reins. When she looked down to thank him, she saw his expression was mournful.

'A sad time, memsahib,' he said.

'Yes; we'll all miss poor Sunil.'

The stable lad looked anxious. 'Do you think there will be trouble for anyone? The new sahib is saying the ladder was not safe, and that Sunil drank too much arrack.'

'Do you mean Sahib Fallowfield?'

'Yes, but none of us believe it's true. Sahib Masham is a good boss and careful, and all of us lads were fond of Sunil. We didn't see him drinking arrack, and if we had, we would have tried to stop him. We wouldn't do anything to harm him.'

'I'm sure you wouldn't. You mustn't worry. I'll speak up for you all if there's any trouble.'

The stable lad thanked her, but from the tone of his voice she wasn't certain that she had reassured him. She wheeled Slipper around and the mare's hooves clattered over the cobbles as they rode off in the direction of the downs beyond the racecourse. She took a different route to her usual one. It would be some time before she could face passing the barn where Sunil's body had been found.

Once on the downs, she gently squeezed her heels into Slipper's flanks until the mare broke into a trot and then a gallop. It was only then that the tears came, driven back into Rose's face by the wind until her cheeks stung and she was half blinded. Close to the place where the ground fell away too sharply for safety, becoming a steep slope of rough grass pitted with holes, she reined Slipper in, and they slowed to a walk. Rose wiped away the tears with the back of her hand, pulled a handkerchief from the pocket of her jerkin and blew her nose. *I must look a terrible sight*, she thought. But what did it matter? Up here there was no one to see her.

Slipper ambled calmly over the lush turf, but Rose's mind was still in a turmoil and her heart was heavy. In her mind's eye she saw the anguish on the face of Sunil's mother when his uncle, Jayasena, had come to the house with the terrible news. Her own mother hadn't wanted her to come out riding this morning, but her father had understood that she needed time alone and encouraged it. Anyway, she wasn't due at work until tomorrow and there wasn't much for her to do at home. Sunil's uncle had seen to the arrangements for his cremation, and the de Silvas, who Jayasena worked for, had given him time off from his duties to be with his sister to comfort her.

Tears welled up again and a lump constricted her throat. It was so unfair. Sunil had never harmed anyone.

Her thoughts turned to the cloud hanging over the race. She had tried to persuade her father to tell her what was going on behind the scenes and eventually he'd agreed to, on condition she kept it to herself. She wondered if Dickie de Jong would really go as far as doping his horses to make money. It was a shocking thought, and he would be foolish to take the risk. But if it was true, it might reflect badly on the racecourse, even if none of the stewards or staff had known anything about it. A confirmed case of doping, combined with the accident, was likely to give the impression that management was sloppy. It would be bad for Pat as well as for the de Jongs.

She thought again of Sunil. It was hard to take in that she would never see him again: grooming Slipper, feeding and watering her, always smiling, and glad to see Rose when she arrived at the stables. Then the excitement of winning the inaugural ladies' race. He had been so proud. Had he really been drunk as Edmund Fallowfield had apparently suggested? She found it very hard to believe.

Calmed by the slow rhythm of Slipper's walk, she started to consider the accident more dispassionately. She remembered how Sunil had seemed very troubled by something when he met her at the stables early on the morning of the race. She should have tried harder to find out what had upset him. If only she hadn't been so preoccupied with what lay ahead, she probably would have done.

It was impossible to believe Sunil would hurt any of the horses himself, but had he chanced to see someone else meddling with either of them? Another memory came back to her of the young man she'd seen coming through the archway that led to the racing stables on her early morning visit. Despite what Toby Heatherington had said about his first visit to the racecourse being for the Hill Country meeting, she was sure he was the man she'd seen. He'd been charming at the Clutterbucks' party but that proved nothing. Suppose he was the person who had tampered with the horses and Sunil had seen him acting suspiciously? He might have decided Sunil needed to be silenced.

An even more awful thought came into her mind; Toby was Eddie's friend. Might Eddie be involved? She knew he was hopeless with money, and putting a lot of money on the horses was just the kind of reckless thing he'd do if he was in debt. He always claimed that the horses he fancied were dead certainties to win – once or twice, she had to admit, he had been lucky — but more often than not, the "dead cert" turned out to be an also-ran. And that was just the times that she knew about.

Sadness gripped her. If Eddie had decided to improve his chances of success by foul means, perhaps encouraged by his friend Toby, much as she didn't want to she had to see him in a very different light. Even more horrible was the thought that he might have been involved in Sunil's death.

She returned to the livery yard where she unsaddled Slipper then rubbed her down and put her back in her box. On the way to her car, she noticed that the door was open to the outhouse that the stable lads used when they had free time. The sound of low voices came from inside. For a moment she hesitated, then decided to go and speak to them. She didn't want to give them the idea that she thought anything about Sunil's death was suspicious, but she might learn something useful.

Inside the outhouse, half a dozen lads sat on the ground in a circle around a large pan of rice and dal. They seemed subdued as they scooped food into their mouths. The one she recognised as the most senior saw her first and scrambled to his feet, swiftly followed by the others. Wiping his hands on his dun-coloured trousers, he said, 'Can we help you, memsahib?'

'Please, carry on with your meal.' Rose gestured that they should all sit again but they remained standing. 'I just wanted to ask you about Sunil. After the racing on Saturday, did he come into town with you?'

'No, memsahib. He never came out with us after a meeting. He always wanted to spend more time with the horses.'

'And then?'

'Then he would go home.'

'So, do you remember what time you left him on Saturday?'

'None of us have a watch, memsahib, but it was after the sun went down.'

One of the lads took a step forward. 'I saw the clock above the office,' he said eagerly.

'What time did it say?"

'I think it was almost seven o'clock.'

'Were you the last to leave?'

They all looked at each other. 'Yes,' said the eldest one eventually. 'The others had already finished their work and gone down. The lights were out in the office.'

'What about any night watchmen?'

There was an awkward silence.

'It's all right,' said Rose. 'I don't want to get anyone into trouble.'

'The owners who don't keep their horses here had taken them away,' said the eldest lad. 'The night watchmen were only going to leave the stables unattended for a little while.'

Rose tried not to show it, but she felt angry. She knew that the festivities after the Hill Country Cup were one of the most popular events in Nuala's calendar, but why had none of the night watchmen stayed behind? If they had done, Sunil might still be alive.

'Do you have any idea how long they were gone?'

The eldest lad shuffled his feet. 'No, memsahib. We are sorry.'

'Never mind. Thank you for your help.'

She had left the shed and was rounding the corner of a nearby barn to return to her car when the tall figure of Edmund Fallowfield brought her up short.

'Miss Appleby! I didn't expect to see you up here today, but it's a great pleasure.'

Rose hoped he hadn't noticed she'd come from the outhouse where the stable lads were having their meal.

'I wanted some fresh air, and a ride seemed the best way to get it.'

He nodded. 'Very wise.' A solicitous look came over his face. 'May I offer my condolences? I believe that you knew the unfortunate young man who died yesterday well.'

61

'Yes, he grew up in my parents' house. His mother is one of our servants. Our mutual love of horses was a bond between us.'

If Fallowfield considered it was an unconventional friendship, at least he was too tactful to show it, thought Rose.

'He'll be a great loss,' Fallowfield went on. 'People who have as strong an affinity with animals as he did are rare. I intend to make it my business to tighten things up around here.'

'What do you mean?'

'Safety and discipline seem to have become rather lax.'

'I've never thought so.'

He smiled. 'I hesitate to contradict a lady, but nevertheless, I think it would be advisable. On a more cheerful note, I've not had the chance to congratulate you on your win. A most impressive performance.'

'It's kind of you to say so.'

'It's the truth, and may I say what a pleasure it was to see the ladies taking part. We should have more of it.'

'I'm afraid not everyone shares your opinion.'

'Sadly not, but perseverance will pay off in the end, I'm sure of it.'

'I'd like to think you're right.'

'Are you going back to town?'

Rose nodded.

'I'd offer you a lift but I'm afraid I have a good deal of work to do.'

'Thank you, but there's no need. I have my car.'

As she drove away, Rose mulled over Fallowfield's implied criticism of Pat Masham. Fallowfield was quite new to his job and perhaps not confident of the security of his position. He might be worried that as he had a position of authority at the racecourse, some of the blame for the accident might attach to him. She doubted that would happen, but it was a fair point that if it were the case, as a new man Fallowfield might be likely to get less sympathy than Pat who had been a trusted stalwart at the stables for thirty years.

Some people took the view that they must attack before they were attacked themselves. Maybe despite his affable manner, Fallowfield was one of them. Or perhaps it was simply that he'd taken a dislike to Pat. If that was the case, she had no intention of helping Fallowfield to make trouble for him. On the other hand, if there was more to Sunil's accident than met the eye, she had to find out the truth.

Her thoughts turned to the evening. She had agreed to go to the cinema with Eddie, and now she wished she hadn't. After everything that had happened, she no longer knew how she felt about him. On the other hand, she didn't want to take the risk of arousing any suspicion on his part, so it would be best to go. Perhaps if she talked about Sunil, she might learn something from how he reacted to the subject.

CHAPTER 6

'I'm so glad you came,' said Eddie as he held the car door open for Rose. 'I was afraid you'd cry off. After what's happened, I wouldn't have blamed you, if you had.'

'I thought about it, I must admit, but then I decided that an outing might take my mind off things.'

'The film looks a good one anyway.'

As they drew up at the cinema, a steady stream of people was going in. The building was far smaller than the cinemas in Colombo but nonetheless attractive. It was cream coloured with a flat roof and an arcaded entrance. A board outside displayed bright posters advertising the film showing that night and future films. In the foyer, a nod to the glamour of Hollywood was provided by a red-plush carpet and some flourishes of gilding on the wrought-iron spiral staircase that led to the balcony. Eddie went to the box office counter and bought their tickets then they headed for the swing doors that led to the stalls, pausing to show their tickets to an usherette on the way.

The lights were down and by the light of her torch, another usherette showed them to their seats. The Pathé newsreel had just begun. As with most of them since war had broken out in Europe, it was dominated by news of the battle to defeat Nazi Germany. One item showed the bulky figure of the British Prime Minister, Winston Churchill, meeting the American president, Roosevelt.

They were sealing an agreement for America to help with the Allied war effort. The scene changed to Iceland where steam gushing from hot springs swirled across the bleak, rocky landscape and American troops were unloading ships bringing much-needed supplies from across the Atlantic to send on to England.

The newsreel ended and the B-film began. When Eddie reached for her hand, Rose's first instinct was to snatch it away, but she resisted and let it remain in his. She must behave as if there was nothing wrong. Glancing sideways, she saw that he was looking at her. She forced a smile before turning back to fix her eyes on the screen, but the jumble of thoughts in her head made it impossible to concentrate on what was happening. As far as she was concerned, the actors might as well have been reciting the telephone directory. All she could think about was Sunil and Eddie. Eddie's behaviour was so normal. Was she being ridiculous even for a moment entertaining the idea that he might have had something to do with Sunil's death?

She thought about Eddie's parents. His mother Grace was an enigma, but Eddie's relationship with her seemed to transcend that and be one of uncomplicated affection, at least on his part. On the other hand, his relationship with his father was complicated. On the surface, Dickie de Jong was charming and amusing, but underneath that she suspected he had a tough disposition. His public criticisms of Eddie were usually couched in jovial terms, although not so much at the Clutterbucks' party, but she knew Eddie well enough to realise that they stung, leaving him wanting his father's approbation but painfully aware that he might never achieve it.

She wondered if Dickie was aware of the pain that he caused his son and didn't care. His and Grace's marriage was a strange one. Dickie often seemed to goad her to provoke a reaction, but if that troubled her, at least in public, she rarely let it show. Sometimes it was as if she treated him as a recalcitrant child who had to be ignored to make them behave. Rumour had it that most of the family's wealth came from her, and that might have had something to do with his behaviour. He probably found the imbalance hard to stomach, even though with his love of luxury and good living, he depended upon it. Perhaps the way he treated Eddie was an outlet for his frustrations.

Once again, she considered what might be going on in Eddie's mind. Had he snapped and given in to the temptation to hit back at his father by colluding with Toby Heatherington to dope Dickie's horses, embroiling him in a scandal? If that was the case and Sunil had witnessed suspicious goings-on, the poor lad might have been nothing more to Eddie than an obstacle to be removed from his path. Her conviction darted from one stance to another and back again. She wanted to believe that Eddie was innocent, but his connection to Toby, and Toby's mysterious visit to the stables, stood in her way.

When the B-film ended, the lights went up a little and trays of tea were brought to the filmgoers in their seats. She only half listened as Eddie talked about what they'd just seen and was relieved when the trays were removed, and the main film began. But once again it was impossible to concentrate on the story; she was none the wiser by the time the lights went up and they emerged with the rest of the audience into the balmy night.

'What do you say to a drink at the Crown?' asked Eddie.

Torn between the tormenting mixture of feelings she was experiencing and the desire to find out more about Toby Heatherington, she nodded. She only hoped that none of her acquaintances would be at the Crown. News travelled fast in a small town like Nuala. Along with gossip about the delay in presenting the Hill Country Cup, she wouldn't be surprised to find that a lot of people had heard about Sunil's accident. The people who knew she had been close to him fell into two camps: those who accepted it as an innocent friendship and those who vehemently disapproved of anything more than a purely master and servant relationship between the locals and the colonial families. She didn't care about the latter, but the sympathy of the former would be almost certain to make her cry.

At the Crown, they went into the bar. To Rose's relief, there were very few other customers, and she knew none of them. As she sat down, the comfortable atmosphere of the mock-Tudor room with its oak panelling and walls papered with William Morris designs soothed her a little. Even in Ceylon, the high-ceilinged room could be chilly on a December evening and a cheerful fire burned in the grate of the huge stone fireplace.

A servant came and Eddie ordered himself a whisky and Rose a martini. When the servant had gone to fetch them, Rose took a deep breath.

'Where's your friend Toby this evening?' she asked in the most casual tone she could muster.

'Oh, he had someone to see about a business matter.'

'He must be a hard worker to give up his evening.'

Eddie grinned. 'I hope you're not implying anything by that.'

Rose clicked her tongue in annoyance. 'Don't be silly. What is your friend's business, by the way? He didn't say when we met at the races.'

Eddie raised an eyebrow. 'You seem very interested in him. Should I be jealous?'

'Probably not, but you don't own me, you know.'

He leaned forward. 'I still haven't given up hope.'

Rose's heart gave a little lurch. For a moment silence fell, then Eddie relaxed into his chair again. 'Bit of a man of mystery actually, old Toby. We were at school together in England but after that we lost touch. Then a couple of months ago he popped up again. Said he was coming to Ceylon and would like to meet up. I thought it would be pleasant to renew an old friendship. But why are we talking about Toby? Don't you like him?'

'On a few minutes' acquaintance how can I answer that?'

Eddie grinned. 'I suppose not. But if you decide you don't, I'll send him packing.'

'I don't think you need go that far,' Rose said with a laugh. She paused. 'It's strange, I could have sworn I saw him up at the stables on the morning of the races. But in the afternoon, he said he'd not been up to the course before.'

'Well, this is his first time in Nuala, and he spent the morning of the meeting away somewhere on business, so that sounds right.' He looked at her crossly. 'Do we have to keep talking about Toby? What's this all about?'

'It's not *about* anything. I was just curious.' She smiled. 'He must have a double.'

Recovering his spirits, Eddie chuckled. 'I'll tell him that. Two fellows with an ugly mug like his must be some kind of record.'

'Oh no, don't!' Rose regretted the words as soon as they were out of her mouth.

'Why not?' asked Eddie irritably.

'Because I've only met him once and it would be rude.'

'But it would be me making the joke, not you. Anyway, Toby has a sense of humour.'

She glowered at him, and he shrugged. 'Oh, very well. I won't say anything.' He finished his whisky. 'I think I'll have another. What about you?'

'No, but don't let me stop you.'

He ordered another glass of whisky and she lapsed into silence, letting him talk until his voice interrupted her thoughts.

'Rose?'

'Sorry, what were you saying?'

'You haven't heard a word, have you? I was trying to tell you about this new business venture some of the chaps at the polo club want me to go into with them. The old man isn't too keen, but I've not given up hope of persuading him.' He looked at her closely. 'You don't think I can make a go of it either, do you?'

'What do I know? But perhaps you should listen to his advice.'

An irritable expression came over Eddie's face. 'You mean listen to him telling me what to do and how stupid my ideas are.' He stared into his whisky glass. 'Although heaven knows why he thinks he has the right to tell other people how to live their lives.'

Rose pushed her glass away. Suddenly, the smell of alcohol turned her stomach, and this was the last place on earth that she wanted to be. 'It's late and I'm tired. Shall we go?'

'If you want.'

A frosty silence hung between them as they drove home. Rose felt as if a stone was pressing on her heart. The evening hadn't helped at all. She was still in a quandary over whether Eddie might have something to do with Sunil's death. If he was innocent, all she'd done was hurt his feelings to no purpose. When they said goodbye, he didn't try to kiss her.

CHAPTER 7

De Silva woke early the following morning and slipped out of bed trying not to wake Jane. In the hall, Billy and Bella appeared from the kitchen quarters and nudged up against his pyjama-clad legs.

'If you want feeding, you'd better go back to the kitchen and find cook,' he said in a whisper.

Bella looked up at him with unblinking green eyes and let out a little miaow.

'Oh, it's the garden that you want, is it?'

In the drawing room, he opened the door to the garden and let the cats out. As he stood and breathed in the cool morning air, they quickly disappeared into the undergrowth. The colour of the sky was moving rapidly from sooty grey to pearl. High above the trees, birds soared in their morning geometry. De Silva wrapped his dressing gown tightly around him and sighed. Usually, he loved to watch the sun come up, but today it was impossible to surrender to the pure pleasure of it. A fitful night's sleep had done nothing to iron out his thoughts about Sunil's death, and if he was to take on the might of the Royal Nuala Jockey Club, he would need some pretty compelling evidence. Henry Fortescue had already made it clear that he didn't expect anything to come of the inquiry into the de Jongs' horses. How much harder it would be to convince him that not only had the horses been doped, but someone had also taken steps to silence a material witness, especially if the man alleged to have been doing the silencing was his deputy, Rupert Wilde. Closing the door, he went back to the bedroom to get dressed. Billy and Bella weren't likely to come back from their morning explorations for a while.

* * *

After breakfasting with Jane on poached eggs and toast followed by slices of mango washed down by several cups of tea, he drove to the station. Prasanna and Nadar were in the public room, so he put them in the picture about everything that had been happening and gave them their instructions.

'I want you to question all the bookies in town,' he finished. 'Find out if any of them accepted large bets on the Hill Country Cup. If so, I want names, or if they can't supply those, descriptions of the people involved.'

'What if the bets weren't placed in Nuala, sir?' asked Prasanna.

'You'll have to go further afield. There are bookies in Hatton and some of the smaller towns that you can try. Take your bicycles, or if it's too far to cycle, go by train. We'll discuss all that if it becomes necessary.'

'Yes, sir.'

They had been gone for some time, and he was wondering whether to return to the stables in case there were any clues that he and Jane had missed when the telephone rang. He picked it up.

'Good morning, de Silva,' said a voice that he recognised as George Appleby's.

'Good morning. What can I do for you?'

'I just thought you'd like to know that those tests came back negative. As I said, it's not absolutely conclusive, but in the light of the fact that they're the best we have available,

Henry Fortescue's indicated to me that he plans to accept them and consider the matter closed. The Hill Country Cup will be awarded to Dickie and Grace de Jong for their horse Bright Star. I'm not sure exactly how Fortescue and the others intend to do it. Maybe under the circumstances a public ceremony would be deemed inappropriate, so there will be a private one then an announcement of some kind in the newspaper. Anyway, I'm relieved that's the club's problem, not mine. I've done my bit.'

De Silva thanked him for the information and put down the receiver. Perhaps, like Henry Fortescue, he should consider the matter – what was the British expression – done and dusted? But he wasn't satisfied that Sunil's death could be so easily explained away as a drunken accident. The question was, how was he going to go about finding out what had really happened?

He looked at his watch; it was nearly midday. Prasanna's and Nadar's inquiries would probably keep them busy for a while longer. He would go home for lunch and talk matters over with Jane. After a quick telephone call to Sunnybank to find out if she was at home, he left the station. It was as he was locking up that he noticed a young woman watching him, and recognised Rose Appleby. She looked as if she wanted to approach him but when he gave her an encouraging smile, she turned and hurried away. He wondered what was on her mind. If it was to talk about a police matter, perhaps she'd come back. It wasn't uncommon for it to take a few attempts before people who wanted to make a complaint to the police worked up the courage to go through with it.

* * *

'What might Rose Appleby want with the police?' mused Jane. 'Are you certain it was her?'

'Definitely, she's hard to miss.' De Silva scooped a spoonful of jackfruit curry and fragrant saffron rice from his plate and put it in his mouth.

'It does seem strange that she changed her mind.' Jane raised an eyebrow. 'Perhaps she thought you looked too forbidding.'

He swallowed his mouthful. 'Slanderous! I am always approachable. Anyway, Rose Appleby doesn't seem the kind of young lady to be easily daunted.'

Jane looked thoughtful for a moment. 'Then perhaps she was afraid of being seen going to the police. I was at church doing the flowers this morning – by the way those lilies I picked from the garden were much admired – and her mother was one of the helpers. She didn't mention anything about Rose having a problem that she needed to see you about.'

'Would Mrs Appleby be likely to confide in you?'

'Oh, I think she might do. After all, she knows I'm your wife.'

'Hmm. So either it's something extremely confidential, or it's something Rose hasn't told her mother, or both. Well, we'll just have to hope that whatever it is, she decides to come back.'

'I know it would be best if she does so of her own volition,' said Jane. 'But do you think you ought to be more active in finding out what's going on?'

'If necessary, but I'll give her time first.'

* * *

De Silva returned to the police station that afternoon and, occupied with a variety of tasks, he thought no more about

Rose Appleby. When he returned home that evening, however, Jane had news for him.

'She telephoned after you left this afternoon. She wants to come and see you.'

'Then why didn't she call the station?'

'Because she doesn't want to meet you there. She wants to come here to Sunnybank.'

'Did she explain why?'

'No, and it clearly wasn't the right time to ask her. She was only on the telephone briefly. She said she was telephoning from her work and had to be quick. I had the impression she was anxious not to be overheard.'

De Silva scratched his chin. 'Well, this is all very mysterious.'

'I suggested she come to tea tomorrow at half past four. I hope you don't mind.'

'Of course not, I'm as interested as you are to find out what she wants to talk about.'

CHAPTER 8

'What a beautiful garden you have,' remarked Rose as she and the de Silvas settled down on the verandah the following afternoon.

'Thank you,' said Jane. 'Although I'm afraid I can't claim any of the credit for it. Shanti's the gardener.'

Rose smiled. 'How lovely. I don't think my parents know anything about gardening. Father's keen on cricket and horse racing, and Mother's always very wrapped up in her amateur dramatics.'

'The world would be a dull place if we were all the same,' said de Silva.

Rose laughed. 'Very true.'

Tea arrived and Jane poured them all a cup then offered Rose some of the butter cake that their servant Leela had brought out. 'Thank you, it looks delicious,' she said, accepting a slice.

De Silva took a slice for himself and put it on his plate. 'Now, how can I help you?'

Rose hesitated. 'You must think it very odd of me to ask to see you in private like this.'

'Not at all. Some matters are sensitive, so it's not a surprise that there are times when people don't want to draw attention to themselves by coming to the police station.'

'Thank you for being so understanding. It's the recent events at the racecourse that I want to talk to you about.

I know from my father that the tests on the de Jongs' two horses came back negative, but I also know that the tests aren't completely reliable.'

There didn't seem to be any point challenging her on that; de Silva nodded.

'Does the name Toby Heatherington mean anything to you?'

De Silva thought for a moment, but Jane spoke first. 'Do you remember, Shanti? We were introduced to him at the party held at the Residence on Hill Country Cup day.'

'Ah yes, a pleasant young man. If I remember rightly, he was a friend of the de Jong family.'

'He's actually a friend of their son Eddie.'

'Why are you interested in him?'

'I'm sure I saw him up at the racecourse early on the morning of the race, but when we met at the party, he denied having been to the course before the afternoon.'

'Yes, I remember it now. He said something about having to go out of town and being worried he wouldn't be back in time. Are you sure you saw him in the morning?'

'I am.'

'And do you have any idea what he was doing?'

'No. If he'd been with Eddie, I wouldn't have thought there was anything suspicious going on. Eddie might just have wanted to show him the horses. But why would Toby go up there on his own, and at such an early hour of the morning?'

'Have you spoken to Eddie about this?'

'Yes, he said that the person I saw couldn't have been Toby. He backed up Toby's story that he'd gone out of Nuala that morning and was visiting the course for the first time on the afternoon of the race. I didn't want to press the point.'

It was possible that Toby hadn't told his friend the truth, thought de Silva, but it had to be considered that Eddie was covering for him.

'Do you recollect the exact time that you saw Toby?' he asked.

'Not to the minute, but it wasn't long after dawn. I often go up early to the stables, and particularly that day because of the ladies' race.'

'And where was he?'

'He was coming through the archway that leads to the looseboxes where horses brought up for the races are kept in readiness. They're often ridden over from their home stables the day before a race, particularly if they have some distance to travel. I called out good morning, but he took no notice of me.'

There certainly was something odd about that, thought de Silva. He didn't imagine that many young men would ignore Rose Appleby. So, either Heatherington hadn't seen her, which meant he must have been extremely preoccupied, or he had deliberately avoided her because he didn't want to talk to anyone and explain what he'd been doing. If it was the latter, it was unfortunate for him that he had a connection to Eddie de Jong and he and Rose had met at the races.

'Were the de Jongs' two horses that were entered in the Hill Country Cup kept at the course overnight?'

'I think they would have been.'

'Was there anyone else about at the stables?'

'Not when I arrived, but Sunil came to find me shortly afterwards. Inspector, I can't help thinking that if Toby tampered with Bright Star and Garnet, and Sunil saw him, Sunil's death wasn't an accident.'

'Yet Sunil didn't say anything to you at the time?'

'No, but he may have been afraid to, or not understood what he was seeing. When I look back on it, he was clearly agitated about something. If I hadn't been so busy thinking about the race, I would have asked him why.' She sighed. 'I wish so badly that I had.'

'Have you spoken to any of the Jockey Club stewards about this?'

Rose shook her head. 'I don't expect they'd be pleased if I suggested they reopen their inquiry. Quite apart from any embarrassment that might cause, they're mostly very traditional in their views on women. My fellow lady jockeys and I had a lot of trouble persuading them to agree to the ladies' race. They're not likely to set much store by my information. I did talk to some of the stable lads, but they just said they'd left Sunil up at the stables when they went to celebrate in town and assumed he'd go home when he was ready.'

De Silva wondered whether a belief that the stewards of the Jockey Club wouldn't listen to her had been the only reason she'd held back from speaking to them. He waited.

Rose took a bite of her butter cake and chewed on it thoughtfully before taking a sip of tea.

She sighed. 'There was another reason why I didn't approach the Jockey Club,' she said at last. 'I've known Eddie since we were children and I've always trusted him. I don't want to make trouble for him unfairly. But I can't get away from the fact that Sunil's dead. He and I grew up together and he was like a brother to me. If he saw something, something that perhaps he didn't fully understand, and was murdered to stop him talking, I need to find that out. And if Toby Heatherington was the person who killed him, I have to face the fact that Eddie might have been a party to the crime.'

Rose looked sad. 'Eddie and his father have a difficult relationship. Eddie's often resentful of the way his father treats him. I'm worried that he might have wanted to pay his father back by making trouble for him. Money might be involved too. Eddie's always short of that.' She glanced at de Silva. 'What will you do now, Inspector?'

'It was brave of you to come to see me. I assure you, what you've told me will be considered and thoroughly investigated. I must insist, however, that from now on, for your own safety, you leave everything to me. Do you promise you'll do so?'

Rose hesitated, uncertainty flickering across her face, then she nodded. 'Very well.'

* * *

'Poor girl,' said Jane when Rose had taken her leave. 'She's obviously very fond of Eddie de Jong. What do you think of her story?'

'I'm satisfied that, as we suspected, we have a murder investigation on our hands, and one that's likely to be extremely unpopular with the higher echelons of Nuala society. In view of that, I think it's unwise to rush into anything. In any case, if this Toby Heatherington is the man that we're after, the last thing we want to do is to arouse his suspicions. Equally, if Rose has already spoken to some of the stable lads, it might cause comment if I turn up asking questions too soon.' He rubbed his chin. 'I think we need a more oblique approach.'

'Such as?'

'I'll ask Prasanna and Nadar if they know any of the stable lads at the racecourse. If they do, they can think of a pretext for asking them casually about this young man Sunil. As Rose was fond of him, she's bound to take a favourable view. I'd like to hear a few more opinions. For example, was he a drinker despite what his family think and was he as conscientious about his job as Rose says he was? Even though she told us there was no one else around when she saw Heatherington, I'd like to be sure of that too. It would also be useful to know if any of the stable lads spotted strangers up at the stables on that or other recent occasions.'

He glanced at his watch and stood up. 'Prasanna and Nadar will have left the station by now, but I'd rather not leave everything until tomorrow. I'll go into town and look for them, but I'll change into civilian clothes first. I'd prefer to attract as little attention as possible.'

CHAPTER 9

De Silva left the Morris near the bazaar and set off through the alleyways in the direction of Prasanna's home. Now that it was dark, the bazaar was deserted except for a few stray cats that scattered into the shadows as he approached, and a couple of skinny, dun-coloured dogs squabbling over discarded food.

In Prasanna's street, lights were on in the windows of the houses. De Silva went up to the one where Prasanna and his family occupied a few rooms and knocked at the front door. Three small boys playing hopscotch on a chalked-out area close by stopped and watched him curiously.

The door opened a few inches and an old man peered out. 'What do you want?'

De Silva ignored his rudeness. 'I'm looking for your neighbour, Prasanna.'

The old man opened the door a few more grudging inches and stood back. 'Second floor.'

De Silva squeezed past him and started to climb the stairs. He had been to the old house before and remembered how the stair treads creaked alarmingly under one's feet. The paintwork was scuffed, and the lights were dim, but appetising aromas of curry reached his nose as he climbed, along with the tempting smell of baking chapattis and naan.

By the time he reached Prasanna's door, the speed of

his heartbeat had increased, and beads of sweat stood out on his forehead. More exercise was needed, he observed regretfully. He knocked and after a moment heard footsteps inside and the sound of a bolt being drawn back. The door opened and Prasanna stood there. He looked surprised at the sight of his boss.

'Sir! I wasn't expecting… Is something wrong? Nadar and I've spoken to as many of the local bookies as possible in the time we've had. We should be finished soon.'

De Silva raised his hand in a gesture of reassurance. 'No need to be alarmed. I'm sure you've done well on that score. If it's not inconvenient, I'd like to speak to you about another matter.'

Prasanna stood aside. 'Please come in, sir.'

The little apartment that Prasanna shared with his wife Kuveni and their daughter was as spotless as it had been on his last visit, its simple furniture brightened by embroidered hangings and cushions that Kuveni had probably made herself. There was, however, no smell of cooking.

'I'm on my own this evening,' said Prasanna apologetically. 'If Kuveni was here, she'd insist you stay to have something to eat with us, but she and our little girl have gone to visit her mother. She's helping Kuveni to get clothes ready for the new baby.'

'Ah yes, it can't be long until the great day.'

Prasanna nodded and de Silva gave him a sympathetic smile. 'You look a little anxious.'

'I'll be glad when it's arrived and they're both safe, sir.'

'Of course, but I'm sure everything will go well.'

'I hope so.'

'If there are any difficulties, you must call Doctor Hebden and tell him I'll pay.'

'That's very kind of you, sir, but we wouldn't want to impose.'

'Nonsense.' He and Jane had become very fond of

Kuveni when she lived with them for a time before her marriage to Prasanna. 'I insist, and so would Mrs de Silva.'

Prasanna's expression brightened. 'Thank you, sir.'

'Now, to the reason I've come.' He explained about Rose's visit and the new light it had cast on the investigation into Bright Star and Garnet, and Sunil's death.

'I'd prefer not to ask any more questions up at the stables, but I hoped that you or Nadar might be able to help. Do either if you know any of the stable lads from the racecourse? If you do, might you be able to talk to them about this lad Sunil? I don't want them to think they're being formally questioned, mind you.'

Prasanna thought for a moment. 'One of them lives near here. I don't know him well, but well enough to strike up a conversation.'

'Does he know that you're a policeman?'

'In this community, sir, almost certainly, but it hasn't stopped us having spoken on friendly terms. Leave it with me, sir. I'll see what I can do, and I'll speak to Nadar.'

'Good, and anything else you can discover about unusual happenings at the stables in the last week or so would be useful.'

* * *

As he drove home, de Silva considered the situation. As yet he had nothing in the way of hard facts to help him. If Prasanna and Nadar found out that Sunil had been partial to a drink, it might mean that alcohol had been a major cause of his fall, but on the other hand, it wouldn't rule out the possibility that someone had deliberately encouraged him to get drunk intending for him to have an accident. Hopefully, his young officers would find someone to throw light on the issue.

Although it would be premature to take Rose's story at face value, when the time seemed right, he must investigate Toby Heatherington. Was his presence in Nuala really just a visit to an old friend? Then there was Rupert Wilde to consider. Maybe his reaction to Fallowfield's remark meant nothing, but it would be interesting to know what his movements had been after the races.

Jane was in the drawing room when he arrived home.

'How did you get on?' she asked.

'A reasonably successful trip. Prasanna says he knows one of the stable lads and will see what he and Nadar can find out. He was on his own this evening as Kuveni and their daughter are at his mother's house. Something about getting clothes ready for the new baby.'

'Yes, it won't be long now.'

'Prasanna was obviously anxious about how everything will go, so I told him to call David Hebden if there are any problems and I'll pay.'

'Good; although naturally one hopes everything will go smoothly.'

'I forgot to ask earlier how your day was.'

'Oh, just the usual kind of thing, you know, and of course there are Christmas events to make plans for too.'

De Silva had almost forgotten it wasn't long until Christmas. He usually went to church with Jane then. Even though he was a Buddhist, he liked to think that Christmas was a festival that the whole community could celebrate together.

There was a knock at the door and their servant Leela came in. 'Shall I tell cook to serve dinner now, memsahib?' she asked.

'Yes please, Leela.'

'What are we having?' asked de Silva as the door closed.

'Curried eggs and a lentil curry with a strawberry jam tart to follow. Cook made the jam with the rest of those strawberries you grew.'

'Excellent, I thought I smelled baking as I came in.' De Silva rubbed his hands. He was happy to eat English food when strawberry jam was involved.

Over dinner, they talked more about the case.

'If Eddie is in financial difficulties,' said de Silva, 'we must consider the possibility that he might be willing to fix a race.'

'But wouldn't he care about harming his family's reputation?'

'We know that he and his father don't get on.'

'There's still his mother to consider.'

De Silva shrugged. 'People in financial trouble often do desperate things.'

He ate another spoonful of his egg curry. The coconut gravy that the eggs swam in was thick and rich, just as he liked it. 'By the way, this is delicious,' he remarked, gesturing to the remaining egg on his plate with his empty spoon. He paused with the spoon still in mid-air. 'Maybe we have to consider the possibility that Dickie de Jong and his wife were involved.'

'Do you really think that's likely? Why would they take the risk? I agree that the odds for Bright Star were much longer than those for Garnet, so someone in the know might have put their money on Bright Star and made a lot of money, but whichever of the de Jongs' horses won, they stood to gain a large prize and the glory of winning.'

'A good point. I'll put them to one side for the moment, but sadly, their son Eddie is a different matter.'

Dinner over, they read and chatted for a while. When they went to bed, de Silva was glad to find that sleep came easily, not something that always happened when his mind was full of a case.

CHAPTER 10

'Now,' said de Silva. 'What have you found out?'

He had arrived early at the station the following morning to find Prasanna and Nadar already there.

Prasanna reached in his pocket and pulled out a notebook. 'We spoke with Anishka, the head stable lad. He's the one who lives near me. He was with a group of the lads he works with. Luckily, they all talked easily about Sunil's accident, so it wasn't too difficult to slip in a few questions. No one seemed suspicious about why we were interested or said anything about us being policemen.' Prasanna grinned. 'That might have had something to do with the fact that we bought a few rounds of arrack.'

De Silva chuckled. 'Just this once you may put in a chit for expenses.'

'Thank you, sir.'

'Anyway, Anishka and the others were all very sure that Sunil didn't drink alcohol. We had the impression that all of them thought the accident was a strange thing to happen.'

'Did you manage to raise the question of foul play?'

'Yes, but they all agreed they couldn't think of anyone who would want to harm Sunil, so perhaps he had been very tired and the rung of the ladder breaking under his weight caught him by surprise. They confirmed that when they'd gone down to town to celebrate, Sunil was left on his own.'

'And what about the staff on duty that day?'

'There were a few grooms who'd come up with their employers' horses but otherwise only the regular staff were there.'

'Had Anishka and his friends met all the visiting grooms before?'

Prasanna consulted his notebook. 'I think so. At least they didn't mention any newcomers. I was wary of asking too many detailed questions and making them suspicious after all.'

De Silva nodded. 'A wise decision. Did you manage to find out if there were any other visitors?'

'Only Mr and Mrs de Jong who came to see their horses before they were saddled up.' Prasanna glanced at his notebook again. 'Anishka said they were accompanied by a man called Edmund Fallowfield. He's the secretary of the Jockey Club.'

'Yes, we've met. So, no mention of anyone that might have been Toby Heatherington. What about security? Is there someone on duty at the stables all the time?'

'Anishka became a bit evasive when I touched on that. We had the impression that not all of the looseboxes were watched all the time.'

'So, someone might have had the opportunity to get to the de Jongs' horses without being seen.' De Silva smiled. 'This is all useful information, well done, both of you.'

* * *

Rose gave up trying to compose her piece on the Nuala Kennel Club's recent dog show and stared into space. She and Eddie hadn't spoken since their evening at the cinema. Usually, he would have telephoned by now to arrange another date. She'd seen him briefly in town and she was sure he'd seen her, but he'd hurried off in the opposite direction.

As the daily business of the office of the *Nuala Times* proceeded at its usual sleepy pace around her, she went back over their last conversation, wincing when she came to the frigid atmosphere in which they'd parted.

The sound of the telephone ringing interrupted her thoughts, and her heart jolted. Perhaps it was Eddie asking if she was free to have lunch with him, and she wasn't sure how to reply. Hesitantly, she picked up the receiver and felt relieved when it was only the editor William Judd's secretary wanting to know when the dog show piece would be ready. She promised it by the end of the morning then put down the telephone.

She read over what she'd typed so far and sighed. Was she right about Florence Clutterbuck's Shih Tzu, Angel? She'd written that he had come second in the toy dog class, but perhaps it had been first. She'd better get that right or there'd be trouble. She consulted her notes − yes, he had come first. Pulling the sheet of paper out of the typewriter, she crushed it into a ball and tossed it into the wire waste-paper basket beside her desk. She was about to put a fresh sheet into the roller when a shadow loomed over her. She looked up to see the *Nuala Times's* news reporter, Jed Fraser, standing in front of her desk.

'Inspiration not flowing this morning, eh?'

'Oh, it will, don't you worry.' She smiled, determined not to let him see her irritation at his patronising tone.

He lowered his voice. 'It had better. Old Judd's on the warpath. His rheumatism must be giving him gyp.'

'Thanks for the warning.'

'My pleasure. Well, I'll be off. People to see and things to do.'

Rose glared at Fraser's retreating back. He was one of those men who clearly didn't think a woman had any place in a newspaper office, or probably in an office at all, except to make the tea, take dictation, or type up letters.

She stared gloomily at the blank page. Reporting on dog and cat shows, flower festivals, and the activities of Nuala's social set hadn't taken long to lose its appeal. She'd loved *His Girl Friday* when it came to the Nuala cinema, but the world it portrayed, one that crackled with excitement, romance, and wisecracks, was a million miles from the world of the *Nuala Times*. Her thoughts went back to Sunil's death. It was ironic that an event that might make dramatic headlines was the last thing she'd ever wanted to happen. She tried to quell the sadness that threatened to overwhelm her and started to type.

By lunchtime she had finished the article. The editor's secretary was out so she left it on her desk with a note and went out to her car. She'd already decided to go up to the stables instead of returning home for lunch as she'd originally intended. She wanted a word with Pat Masham. If anyone knew what went on up there, he did. She wouldn't mention Toby or Eddie, but she would ask if he'd noticed any strangers at the stables on race day. Luckily, her mother had been out when she called home to say she wouldn't be there for lunch after all, so there'd been no need to explain herself.

As she drove, she thought of her visit to de Silva. Had she been wrong to talk to him? What if she'd made a mistake about Toby Heatherington and it was someone else that she'd seen up at the stables that morning? Eddie would have every right to be angry with her if she'd traduced his friend and it would be even worse if he guessed that she might have been tarring him with the same brush.

She wiped away a tear. Perhaps she'd telephone him when she finished work this afternoon. But then what would she say if he was still angry and raised the subject of Toby? She could hardly tell him that she suspected his friend was a murderer.

Some of the stable lads were mucking out looseboxes

when she arrived, wheeling the barrowloads of dirty straw to a steaming silage heap. She found Masham in one of the barns nailing back a loose board. It was noticeable that he wasn't his usual friendly self.

'I've told the police everything I know,' he grumbled when she raised the subject of the accident. 'I've nothing to add.' He gave the nail he was using to fix the board another bash with his hammer, hit his finger in the process and cursed under his breath then mumbled an apology. 'I'm sorry about young Sunil,' he went on. 'I know how fond of him you were. He didn't deserve to have something like that happen to him, but I won't take the blame. I've always made sure that everything up here's kept in good order. Fallowfield can say what he likes about the way I run the place. What does he know? Only been here five minutes and thinks he's the expert. I've been thirty years around horses and stables. Accidents happen, even in the best run organisations, and they're no one's fault.'

Rose put a hand on his shoulder. 'If he thinks you're in the wrong, I'm sure he's the only one who does, Pat.'

'It's kind of you to say so, but I wouldn't be too sure.'

'Has anyone else criticised you?'

'Not to my face.'

'Well, there you are. I'm sure men like Henry Fortescue and Rupert Wilde wouldn't hesitate to say something if they thought you were to blame.'

Masham grunted. 'I suppose you're right.'

'Of course I am.' She hesitated. 'Pat, please don't take this badly but it's occurred to me that there might be more to Sunil's death than meets the eye.'

'What do you mean?'

'I'm not blaming you, but just suppose someone tampered with that ladder. A person who wanted to silence Sunil because he'd seen them doing something they shouldn't.'

Masham frowned as he thought for a moment. 'Is this about the business with Garnet and Bright Star?'

'Yes. I know from my father that the tests came back negative, but he admits they aren't completely reliable. Suppose the horses were drugged after all and Sunil witnessed it. Did you notice anything unusual or see any strangers at the stables on the morning of the Cup, or did Sunil mention anything to you or seem worried?'

Masham put down the hammer. 'No. Now listen, Rose, Sunil's death was a tragedy to be sure, but it was an accident, and there's been enough trouble already.'

'I want to believe you, Pat, but I'm still not sure.'

He shook his head, a sad expression on his face. 'You be careful, Rose. I don't believe anything funny's been going on but if I'm wrong about that, it's a job for the police.'

'I've already spoken to Inspector de Silva.'

'What did he say?'

'That if there was anything about Sunil's death that needed investigating, he'd deal with it. In other words, I mustn't interfere.'

Pat shrugged. 'There's your answer. Best to leave it to the police.'

He was a good man, thought Rose, and she'd always liked him. Despite his frequently gruff manner, he cared about the horses and his staff. She felt sure he spoke in good faith, so she didn't press the point, but if he wouldn't help her, and Inspector de Silva refused to tell her anything, she'd have to find a way of discovering what really happened on her own.

'Perhaps you're right,' she said with a sigh, 'and I'm just clutching at straws. I'll leave you to get on with your job. They're expecting me back at work this afternoon and I'd like to see Slipper before I go.' She paused. 'Pat, I'd be grateful if you wouldn't mention to anyone that we've spoken.'

'Very well.'

When she reached Slipper's loosebox, the mare craned her head and whinnied. Rose stroked her cheek. 'Have you missed me?' Slipper tossed her head, dislodging a fly that had settled on a streak of moisture leaking from one of her eyes. 'You probably care much more about seeing me than Eddie does,' Rose added sadly.

She was lost in her thoughts when a voice behind her made her jump. She turned to see Edmund Fallowfield standing a few paces away.

'I'm sorry, I didn't mean to startle you.'

'There's no need to apologise.'

He gestured to Slipper. 'She's looking well.'

'Yes, she is.'

He took a step closer. 'Look, I hope I'm not speaking out of turn but just now I passed the barn where Masham was working. I couldn't help hearing you say something to him about talking to the police. Was it about your friend Sunil?' Fallowfield waited for her to speak then when she didn't, he continued, 'Masham and I don't get on, so I didn't join you and decided to speak to you privately. I suspect we may be thinking along the same lines.'

'What do you mean?' Rose looked at him warily. She hardly knew this man and she was far from sure that she wanted to confide in him, especially if he didn't like Pat.

'I'm sorry if the subject distresses you, but I believe there was more to Sunil's death than meets the eye. I think you do too. I've considered speaking up, and if you've already approached the police, it would be helpful to know the upshot of your conversation.'

'You don't think it was an accident either?' Rose asked quickly.

'No, and although I wouldn't expect him to believe me, I've regretted suggesting that Masham was at fault. The drinking is a different matter. Sunil may have been tricked into that with a view to making him fall.'

'Who would want to do that?' asked Rose cautiously. Part of her didn't want to hear the answer in case he mentioned Eddie.

'Someone who thought Sunil had evidence that they'd tampered with those horses in the Hill Country Cup. I have my eye on Rupert Wilde.'

Inwardly, Rose breathed a sigh of relief.

'I've reason to believe he has money troubles. A man in that position might be tempted to bend the rules. It's plausible he'd have enough knowledge to enable him to tamper with horses and no doubt have opportunities to obtain the means. His presence here would be unlikely to arouse suspicion. I believe it's possible that poor Sunil witnessed something and if I'm right about Wilde, he decided the lad must be silenced. Of course one can't discount other suspects. The de Jongs, for example. Due to Bright Star's unexpected success, they may have benefitted to a greater degree than they would have done if Garnet had won the cup.'

Rose tensed again and Fallowfield looked at her closely. 'I'm sorry, I've distressed you.'

'No.' Rose tried to keep her voice steady.

'What did the police have to say?'

'I spoke to Inspector de Silva. He told me that if anything needed to be investigated, he would deal with it.'

'Hmm, I heard he was up at the stables again. His reaction doesn't sound very encouraging, but I won't let that put me off trying to find out what's been going on. I appreciate it may be harder for you. All I ask is that if you do find out anything, you share it with me. I promise to do the same for you.' He smiled. 'I think we have a lot in common, Rose. We both have inquiring minds and determined natures. I believe we'll make a good team.'

CHAPTER 11

The next morning de Silva and Jane were having breakfast when a call came from the Residence.

'Archie wants to see me,' he said when he returned to the dining room. 'It might be something unconnected with Sunil or the de Jongs and their horses, but I have an uncomfortable feeling that it won't be. Of course, it would have been necessary to speak to Archie at some point, but I'd hoped to be further forward in the investigation before I did so.'

Jane gave him a sympathetic smile. 'I think we found enough evidence at the barn to stop him from telling you to back off, quite apart from what Rose had to tell us.'

'I'd like to think so.'

'But do finish your meal before you go. Cook's making French toast. We had some bread that needed using up.'

'Ah, then Archie will have to wait,' said de Silva with a smile. He was very partial to French toast, which Jane had explained to him was not really French at all and had probably been eaten as far back as the days of the Ancient Romans. In England it had once gone by the quaint name of Poor Knights of Windsor. Unlike Jane's green juice, he doubted it had any health benefits, unless you counted the ability of delicious food to lift the spirits.

* * *

The Residence was busy with servants going about their morning duties. A small team of gardeners was raking the gravel on the front drive and cutting the lawn that bordered it. Two servants were up ladders, washing the windows on the big house's upper floor. At the ground-floor windows below, other servants were also busy with buckets of soapy water and cloths.

Florence met him in the reception hall, her beloved Shih Tzu Angel tucked under one arm.

'Good morning, Inspector,' she trilled. 'Such a busy one. We have guests coming up from Colombo tomorrow.' She broke off as a female servant appeared, carrying a large crystal-glass vase filled with pink and white lilies.

'Put those over there.' Florence pointed to a side table between two windows. When the vase had been placed, she marched over to scrutinise it.

'A little to the right.'

The servant hurried to adjust the vase.

Florence nodded. 'Yes, that will do.' With a disapproving expression on her face, she examined the window to her left.

'This hasn't been properly washed. There are smears on it. Tell one of the men to clean it again.'

The servant scuttled away on her errand, and de Silva watched her retreating back with sympathy. He wouldn't want to be in the Residence servants' shoes when Florence was in this kind of mood. The visitors must be very important.

Florence frowned. 'How everything will be ready in time, I don't know. This visit coming on top of the celebrations for the Hill Country Cup has been most inconvenient.' She looked genuinely agitated and de Silva found himself feeling a little sorry for her. He knew she had a good heart under the bossy exterior, and there was no harm in wanting to show off Nuala at its best.

'I mustn't keep you,' Florence went on. 'I expect you've come to visit my husband. I last saw him in his study.'

De Silva thanked her and headed for the familiar corridor lined with hunting prints that led to Archie's bolthole. He stopped at the well-polished mahogany door and knocked, then hearing Archie's voice call out, went in. Darcy, Archie's elderly Labrador, ambled over to greet him, tail wagging as usual.

Archie raised an eyebrow. 'I see that you managed to run the gauntlet. How are things going out there?'

It's as if I came from the field of battle, thought de Silva with amusement, *not just the reception hall*. 'Mrs Clutterbuck tells me you're preparing for visitors.'

'My brother and his wife.'

De Silva was surprised that a family visit was causing such consternation.

'Between ourselves, there's a bit of rivalry between my wife and my sister-in-law. It's just as well they don't live in the same town all the time.'

That explained it, thought de Silva. A hive needed only one queen bee.

'Luckily, my brother's as fond of fishing as I am,' Archie went on. 'We spent hours messing about on the river when we were boys, fishing from the bank or taking out the little rowing boat we were allowed to use, so we'd have an excuse to make ourselves scarce.'

De Silva tried to conjure up a picture of Archie as a boy, messing about on the river. It was quite difficult when one was used to his tall, bulky figure, grey hair, and craggy features. He wondered what Archie's brother would be like.

'It's a pity they couldn't get up here a few days earlier – my brother's a keen racing man and he would have enjoyed the Hill Country Cup meeting – but duty called. Like me, he's in the colonial service. Now, to business. I've had a call from Edmund Fallowfield, the secretary of the

Jockey Club. Henry Fortescue told me you met him on race day when Hebden was taking samples from the de Jongs' horses, and Fallowfield himself said you met again in connection with an unfortunate accident at the stables where a young man died. Fallowfield has the idea that you're making further inquiries into the accident, and he wants to know what's up.'

De Silva groaned inwardly. He'd known he'd have to talk to Archie about his suspicions, but he'd hoped to keep the matter between the two of them. Had he and Jane been spotted after all when they visited the stables? He feared it was the case.

'Did Mr Fallowfield say what made him think there were to be further inquiries?'

'He didn't specify. I told him that most likely you just need to check a few details for the report that's customary when there's an accidental death,' Archie went on. 'But you know these types that like to play amateur detective. He also has an idea about the result of those tests that Hebden sent off to be analysed being unreliable and there being some kind of skulduggery going on. He suggested Rupert Wilde or Dickie de Jong might be involved. Wilde in particular, who has, Fallowfield suspects, been betting heavily on the horses and may be in serious difficulties over money. I didn't want to encourage Fallowfield, so I decided to stave him off until I'd had the chance to speak to you.'

He levelled a knowing look at de Silva. 'I hope you're going to tell me that you're just tidying things up and Fallowfield's indulging in fantasies, but I have a nasty feeling in my bones that you're not.' He reached for the packet of Passing Clouds on his desk, shook one out and lit it. 'So, you'd better tell me what's going on.'

'I'm afraid I'm not able to set your mind at rest, sir. I believe that the young man Sunil's death may not have been an accident.'

'Are you suggesting he was murdered?' Archie asked sharply.

There was a look of concern on his face. He listened whilst de Silva explained about the circumstances in which Sunil's body had been found and what he and Jane had subsequently discovered, then shook his head. 'Are you sure this ladder that the lad's body was found under was tampered with?'

'I am, sir, and I have it on good authority that Sunil didn't drink. If he'd had any alcohol that evening, it would be out of character.'

'What else have you found out about him?'

'Everyone I've spoken to so far has been unable to think of a reason why anyone would want to hurt him.'

'So, what's your conclusion?'

'I think there may be a connection to the alleged doping of the de Jongs' horses. George Appleby had already mentioned to me that the tests he conducted aren't necessarily reliable, so the horses might still have been drugged. If Sunil chanced to see who did it, they would have wanted to silence him.'

'This is sad and troubling news,' said Archie with a sigh. He thought for a moment. 'If there's still a question mark over the result of the Hill Country Cup, the Jockey Club will eventually need to be informed. Of course, they won't like it if we throw a spanner in the works. As far as Henry Fortescue and his chaps are concerned, the inquiry is done and dusted, but if it has to be reopened, so be it. What about Wilde and Dickie de Jong? Do you buy Fallowfield's theory that one of them is involved?'

De Silva gave him the gist of the story that Rose had told to him and Jane.

'I don't have a lot of time for Dickie de Jong,' said Archie when he'd finished. 'Far too full of himself, but if you're right about his son, one has to feel sorry for him.

A betrayal like that would be a terrible blow to any father. As for Heatherington, I agree we need to find out more about him. I'll see what I can do at my end. I believe I heard something about his being a naval man. If he's based at Trincomalee, which seems the most likely, I have a few contacts who may be able to throw light on him.'

'Thank you, sir.'

'We'll have to think what to do about Wilde. I can tell you a bit about him. He was regular army but came out of it about five years ago. Under a bit of a cloud, it seems. Something to do with a fellow officer's wife. Since then he's dabbled in various ventures including a stake in a rubber plantation and a club in Kandy that folded after a year. If Fallowfield's right that he's strapped for cash, he may have given in to temptation. On reflection, in view of Wilde's position with the Jockey Club, quite apart from any other considerations, we'd better keep Fortescue and the others in the dark for the moment.'

'Very well, sir.'

'Did this lad Sunil have a family?'

'His mother works for the Appleby family and his uncle is one of my servants.'

'See to it that any appropriate assistance is offered, will you?'

'Certainly.'

'What about Rose Appleby?'

'She's agreed to leave everything to me.'

'Good.' Archie stubbed out the remains of his cigarette. 'So, I think we're done for now, de Silva. Do keep me up to speed.'

De Silva got to his feet. 'Of course, sir.'

Archie chuckled. 'And good luck getting out of here unscathed.'

CHAPTER 12

'We finished talking to the last of the bookies this morning, sir,' said Prasanna. 'None of them could recall any unusually large bets being made on Bright Star.'

Nadar, who stood beside him in de Silva's office with the afternoon sun filtering through the window, nodded. 'Or any of the other horses in the Hill Country Cup, sir.'

'I'm sure you've done your best.' De Silva sat back in his chair and considered his next move. 'I think it's time to widen the net. I'll have a word with Inspector Singh over at Hatton.'

'Shall I get him on the telephone?' asked Nadar.

'Just make sure he's available to see me then I'll go down in person.' The drive to Hatton was always a pleasant one and it would blow the cobwebs away. Perhaps it would also help to dispel the frustration he felt at the lack of progress in the case. It wasn't Prasanna's or Nadar's fault, but their report hadn't lifted his spirits.

After Nadar had ascertained that Singh would be able to see him, he left his junior officers in charge of the station and set off. The Hatton road snaked through countryside dominated by tea plantations. On all sides, rolling hills cloaked with the vibrant green of tea bushes stretched into the blue distance. The tops of some of the hills were veiled in a light mist. Here and there, the silvery gleam of a waterfall caught the eye.

Hatton came into view and the road descended a little, still twisting and turning, affording views of the shining waters of the lake that lay on the other side of the town. It was considerably larger than the lake in Nuala and wilder with numerous trees around it. The town was also larger than Nuala, with many more substantial bungalows and houses than one saw at home, as well as several more temples.

On the final stretch of road leading into town, he came up behind a convoy of bullock carts taking huge bundles of tea to the market. Thanks to the carts and the increasing amount of other traffic, he was forced to slow down, and it took him another ten minutes to reach the police station.

It was larger than Nuala's, housed in a single-storey building with whitewashed walls punctuated by black columns. De Silva was aware that it was also a lot busier. Singh had around a dozen men at his disposal whereas he had only Prasanna and Nadar. He hoped Singh would be able to spare some of them at short notice.

When de Silva was shown into his office, Singh got to his feet. He was a tall, sinewy man, dressed in crisply ironed khaki shorts and tunic, topped by a white turban. His sharply contoured, bearded face habitually looked severe but today it was softened by a smile.

'Good morning, my friend. It's always a pleasure to see you. I hope nothing serious has brought about this urgent visit.'

'A pleasure to see you too, but regrettably that's not my only reason for coming.'

'Naturally.' Singh gestured to a chair. 'Please, take a seat. I'll have some tea brought and you can tell me about your problem.'

Over cups of the strong, spicy tea that Singh favoured, de Silva outlined the facts of the case so far. 'My men have exhausted the possibilities amongst the bookies in Nuala. I was hoping you would be able to spare some of your fellows to ask around in Hatton,' he finished.

'Of course. Happy to help.' Singh reached for a notebook and pen. 'So, the men you're interested in are Rupert Wilde, Toby Heatherington, and Eddie de Jong.'

'Yes, and Eddie's father Dickie, too,' he added as an afterthought. After all, Dickie's finances were alleged to be unsound, and the winner's prize would probably have to be shared with his wife, not all kept for himself. 'But I'd be glad to know about anyone who placed large bets.'

Singh wrote down the men's names. 'Descriptions?'

De Silva described them, and Singh wrote down that information too.

'Is there anything else I can help you with?'

'Not for the moment.'

'Good.' Singh closed his notebook and put the cap back on his pen. 'Well, I'll be in touch. I hope in a day or two.'

De Silva thanked him and took his leave. As he passed through the public room, three times as busy and noisy as Nuala's, he thought how glad he was that he had chosen the posting to his little town. If Hatton was anything to go by, Colombo was probably a bear pit by now.

Driving through town by a different route back to the Nuala road, he passed the large bazaar. Its multitude of fruit and vegetable stalls displayed a patchwork of colour, from watermelons sliced open to reveal the scarlet flesh inside their lizard-green skins, to purple aubergines, and pillowy bundles of fresh herbs. Stalls selling clothes, household goods, trinkets, and brightly gilded votive pictures and statues were decorated with garlands of paper flowers. Cows wandered along the streets unhindered, dodged by rickshaws, bicycles, and pedestrians. There was a smell of spices and the sound of stallholders shouting out exhortations to buy their wares. It was a lively scene and full of colour, but once again, de Silva reflected that he preferred Nuala's more sedate pace of life.

Eventually he left the streets behind and emerged onto the country road once more. The journey back to Nuala seemed shorter than the one down to Hatton. It was strange how that was often the case. At the station, he spoke briefly to Prasanna and Nadar, but they had nothing new to report. He told them to go home and shortly after that left for home too. It hadn't been a very satisfactory day, but at least he had a good dinner to look forward to.

* * *

'Did you have a productive day?' asked Jane.

'I'm not sure that's really how you'd describe it.'

'I'm sorry to hear that.'

He explained about what he'd learned from his visit to Archie and the report he'd had about the betting on the Hill Country Cup from Prasanna and Nadar.

'I wonder what tipped Fallowfield off about your investigation,' mused Jane.

'According to Archie, he didn't say, and I can hardly ask him. It might give the game away. But I suspect we were spotted when we went to search the barn. On the plus side, I subsequently drove down to see Singh, and he's agreed to put some of his men onto checking with his local bookies.'

'Well, that's progress, isn't it?'

'I suppose it is. How did your day go?'

'I spent most of it preparing for the Sunday school's Nativity play. Poor Mrs Peters has been under the weather, and I've been asked to help out.'

'I hope it's nothing serious.' De Silva had always liked the vicar's wife. She was shrewd but kind and seemed to have the happy knack of bridging religious divides.

'Oh, I don't think so. She just needs time to rest.'

In the dining room, their servant Leela brought dishes

of jasmine rice, jackfruit curry, crispy chicken in an aromatic sauce, and a pile of buttery paratha bread.

'Going back to Edmund Fallowfield's visit to Archie,' said Jane as they ate. 'I wonder why he went to the Residence rather than coming to you.'

'Maybe because the British like to stick together. Present company excepted, of course.'

'Do you think he'll leave it at that?'

'Who knows? I think that will rather depend on how convincing Archie managed to be. He didn't want to encourage Fallowfield, so I believe he gave him pretty short shrift, but if he does come to me, he might have something interesting to impart.'

'Will you go and speak to Wilde and the others?'

'I've not decided yet. Perhaps I can glean information some other way.' He helped himself to some more jackfruit curry. 'One thing's for sure, I'm looking forward to this weekend. A couple of days in the garden are just what I need.'

'And it's no more than you deserve.' Jane held out the basket of paratha bread. 'Why not have another piece of this to go with your curry?'

CHAPTER 13

On Monday morning, de Silva hadn't been at the police station long when Nadar came in to tell him that he had a visitor.

'Does he have a name?'

'Yes, sir. He says he is Sahib Fallowfield.'

'You'd better show him in.'

He got to his feet and wished Fallowfield good morning. The Secretary's smile was polite but cool as he returned the greeting.

'What can I do for you?' asked de Silva.

'I imagine that by now the assistant government agent has had a word with you. I went to see him to find out what's going on. Peter Findley, our clerk of the course, saw you up at the racecourse again last week. He was about to come and ask if you needed help, but you drove off before he had the chance.'

'If I'd known he was there, I would have waited. I didn't see any cars in the yard.'

'Oh, Findley always parks at the back of the offices to take advantage of the shade. Poor fellow spends his life trying to keep out of the sun.'

De Silva remembered the clerk of the course's pale freckled complexion and sandy hair.

'Mind if I smoke?'

De Silva shook his head. Fallowfield produced a lighter

and a pack of cigarettes from his pocket, took one out and lit it, cupping his hands around the flame as he did so. 'Now, as I said, what I'd like to know is why you were at the racecourse again.'

'As I believe Mr Clutterbuck suggested to you, it was a routine visit to enable me to file the report that's customary in the case of an accidental death.'

'I'm not a fool, Inspector. I'm well aware that you're unable to discuss police business with a member of the public, but if there's something amiss, and I have a strong suspicion that there is, I may be able to help you.'

'Oh?'

'As I mentioned to your boss, although unfortunately he didn't seem very interested in hearing my reasons, I think it would be advisable for you to take a good look at Rupert Wilde.'

'The deputy chairman of the Jockey Club?'

Fallowfield nodded.

'Why would I do that?'

'Because I've had my suspicions about him for some time. I believe he's been betting a lot of money on the horses. Wilde enjoys a very expensive lifestyle but apart from his role in the Jockey Club, which I know doesn't pay him much, and dabbling in various business projects when the mood takes him, I fail to see how he supports it. Of course, he may have family money to fall back on, but that's only surmise. I know nothing about his background. No doubt you're aware that drug tests on horses aren't entirely dependable. I believe the fact that Garnet and Bright Star were given a clean bill of health doesn't mean to say that's the end of the matter.'

De Silva was puzzled. Why would Fallowfield persist in making a case for the Jockey Club's inquiry being unreliable when the club was his employer? After all, such behaviour might even jeopardise his job. Was it out of a sense of moral duty or did he have a personal reason for bearing a grudge against Rupert Wilde? Once again, de Silva remembered Wilde's reaction to Fallowfield's joke. Had he hit a raw nerve, or was Wilde's reaction just connected to his reputation with the ladies? Maybe Fallowfield was envious and had hoped to embarrass Wilde by alluding to that in the company of Wilde's superior, perhaps with some success.

'What are you suggesting, Mr Fallowfield?'

'I'm suggesting that those horses were tampered with before the Hill Country Cup was run, and Rupert Wilde was involved.' He gave de Silva a keen look. 'I also think it's not beyond the bounds of possibility that the horses' owner, Dickie de Jong, knows something about the business. De Jong is another one who's profligate with money, but in his case, it's pretty clear it comes from his wife.'

'Mr de Jong would be taking a considerable risk.'

Fallowfield laughed. 'Oh, I don't think that would deter him. He has a reputation for being reckless. Fast cars, gambling, and other activities if you take my meaning. One wonders how much that wife of his knows. Hard to tell what goes on in her pretty head.'

He looked questioningly at de Silva. 'Well, do you have anything to share with me? If you're investigating that young man Sunil's death, I'd be interested to know more.'

'I'm much obliged to you for coming in, sir. What you've told me will be noted, but to be frank, unless you have any hard evidence, all this is surmise.'

'Surmise based on observation, Inspector,' answered Fallowfield sharply. 'And I assure you, I'm an acute observer.'

'I'm sure you are, sir, but observation is one thing and hard evidence another. As I said, I'm grateful for the information. I assure you, anything that needs investigation will receive it, but it would be best for you to take no further action. In the event there has been criminal activity, of which we currently have no proof, you might be putting yourself in danger.'

Fallowfield smiled dryly. 'Kind of you to be concerned for my welfare, Inspector. Have no fear, I won't do anything ill-advised.'

'I'd prefer that you did nothing at all, sir.'

'Are you suggesting the Jockey Club should be kept out of the picture?'

'Not in so many words, but I believe that the time to inform the club is after any wrongdoing is established, not before.'

'And establishing it is the job of the police, eh?'

'Exactly.'

Fallowfield stubbed out his cigarette in the clean ashtray on de Silva's desk then stood up and held out his hand. De Silva shook it. The palm was cool and dry; he noticed that Fallowfield's fingers were deeply stained with nicotine.

'Good afternoon to you, Inspector. It's been a pleasure. If you should change your mind, call on me at any time.'

After the door had closed behind him, de Silva shook his head. Fallowfield was a strange fellow. He looked forward to telling Jane about the visit when he got home.

* * *

That afternoon, Rose was working on an article for the following weekend's Sunday edition of the *Nuala Times*. The editor had decided it would be timely to include a feature on the role of women doing war work. Under normal circumstances, it was a subject that she would have found interesting. Back in Britain, the war was making a great difference to the lives of many women who were doing their bit to support the war effort in hospitals and factories, and on farms. Since her conversation with Edmund Fallowfield, however, she was finding it even harder than before to concentrate on anything.

Fallowfield hadn't been in touch, and she wasn't sure what to make of it. Did it mean he'd given up on the idea that the result of the Jockey Club's inquiry had been incorrect, and Sunil's death hadn't been an accident? Or had he found out something that he didn't want her to know?

She glanced up at the clock. There was an hour to go before the office closed but it was very quiet. Jed Fraser was out, ostensibly on the trail of a story about a new reservoir being built to the west of town, but as the sports reporter was also out and there were no sporting events in Nuala that day, she suspected that the closest they'd got to a story was their favourite bar. The editor's wife was unwell, and he had gone home early, followed shortly by his secretary.

Rose pushed her hair back from her forehead. Two of the fans in the main room's ceiling hadn't been working for the past few days and it was hotter than usual. She worked extra hours when it was necessary. No one ought to blame her if she left a little early. Taking the unfinished article out of her typewriter, she put it to one side and straightened her desk. She was about to go out to the small washroom that she had managed to claim for her own use, when the office telephone rang. She got up and went over to answer it, an uncomfortable feeling coming over her when she heard Fallowfield's voice. What if he'd given up on the idea that Wilde might be responsible and was turning his attention to the de Jongs as he'd suggested he might? She wished now that she hadn't encouraged him that day at the stables. She could simply have told him that he'd misheard her conversation with Pat.

'I'm sorry I've not been in touch before,' he said. 'I decided to sound out Archie Clutterbuck and that police inspector about any investigations into the doping and Sunil's sad demise. I suppose one shouldn't be surprised that they were distinctly unresponsive, but unfortunately it leaves us no further forward. What do you say to meeting up to discuss ideas about where to go from here? Not in Nuala, of course. That would attract attention, but I can pick you up when you finish work. We could drive out to the country.'

Rose's brow furrowed as a suspicion came into her mind. Was Fallowfield really interested in finding out the truth about the de Jongs' horses and Sunil, or was all of this an excuse to get to know her better? She remembered the way he'd suggested that they had a lot in common and would make a good team. He hadn't really known Sunil. No one would blame him for not getting involved.

'I'm sorry,' she said quickly, 'but that's not possible. I have another engagement.'

'I see.' He sounded disappointed. 'Then we must talk another time.'

'Yes, I'm sorry but I have to go now.' To her dismay, as she put the receiver back in its cradle, she found that her hand was shaking. Her excuse had been awkward and abrupt; she wished she had handled the conversation better.

CHAPTER 14

After breakfast the next morning, de Silva kissed Jane goodbye and went out to the Morris. He stopped for a moment to admire his beloved car. Freshly washed and polished by Jayasena, her smart navy paintwork and chrome sparkled in the morning sunshine. He was about to open the driver's door when he felt something brush against his leg and looked down to see Bella gazing up at him expectantly. He smiled. 'So you fancy coming to the station with me, do you?'

Bella gave a little miaow and he bent to pick her up, stroking her glossy black fur. 'I don't think police work is for cats.' He took her over to the front door and put her down gently. 'Much better to spend the day here. But don't get up to too much mischief whilst I'm away.'

It would be nice to have nothing to do but join Bella on one of her morning rambles around the garden, he thought, as he drove to the station. Instead, he had a morning of waiting for news from Inspector Singh, and hopefully Archie, that might help to bring him closer to an answer. Yesterday evening, he and Jane had discussed the latest development and agreed that Fallowfield's behaviour was odd. It was tempting to dismiss the man's allegations as being motivated by spite, but it was always best to leave no stone unturned. It looked as if the odds of solving the case quickly were still long.

With a sigh he thought of the mountain of paperwork that was accumulating in his in-tray. The British! With their love of rules and regulations, and documenting everything, there was always plenty of that. Permits, licences, reports: there were forms to complete for everything, and often of course, a fee to be paid. He wondered if that would change if the British left Ceylon. Somehow, he doubted it. He'd always thought that bureaucracy was a little like Pinocchio's nose. If the simplification of a process was promised, it usually resulted in quite the opposite outcome; one that was lengthier and more complicated.

He slowed and changed into second gear to pass a large white cow that was ambling along the road, its dewlap swinging gently under its neck and its hide rippling over its bony flanks. As he drew level, de Silva steered the Morris towards the crown of the road. Those horns might be short, but they were sharp, and occasionally a cow took exception to a car that came too close. The fault, however, was always considered to be with the motorist. Cows were held sacred by Hindus and must be allowed to roam where they pleased.

He left behind the leafy streets and reached the centre of town. At the station, Prasanna and Nadar were already in the public room.

'Have there been any calls?'

'Not yet, sir.'

'I suppose it's still early.'

'Are you hoping to hear from Inspector Singh, sir?' asked Nadar.

'Yes. If he calls, put him straight through, will you? Mr Clutterbuck might also call.'

He gave the two young men some tasks for the morning and went to his office. An hour had passed when the telephone rang. He picked up the receiver.

'Inspector Singh for you, sir,' said Nadar.

'Put him on.'

Singh's deep voice rumbled down the line wishing him good morning. 'I'm afraid I haven't anything to tell you that will magically solve your case,' he went on.

'I'm sorry to hear that.'

'What I can tell you is that your man Eddie de Jong is deeply in debt to some of the bookmakers over here, but he didn't have any bets with them on the Hill Country Cup. In fact, most of them said they've refused to take his bets until they see the colour of his money.'

De Silva rubbed his chin. That was interesting. It indicated that even if Eddie had been party to doping the horses, he would have had difficulty benefitting from his crime. Of course, that didn't mean that his friend Toby Heatherington would be similarly handicapped.

'No one recognised the name,' said Singh when he asked about Heatherington. 'But someone laid a five hundred rupee bet on Bright Star to win the Hill Country Cup.'

'Phew! That's quite a sum. Did your men get a description of this person?'

'I'm afraid not. The bookmaker said all Britishers look alike to him.'

'Ah well, it's something to know that it was a Britisher. That's assuming the man has anything to do with my case.'

'I'm sorry we haven't found out something more useful for you.'

'No need to apologise. I'm most grateful for your help.'

'I'll be in touch if anything else comes up.'

De Silva thanked him and put down the receiver. He picked up his pen and made a few notes then settled back in his chair to think. The fan suspended from the ceiling hummed, stirring the heavy air; from outside came the faint noise of traffic. With one finger, de Silva traced the pale groove of a scratch on the top of his wooden desk. He feared the case was still a long way from being solved. If Eddie de Jong and Toby Heatherington were the villains, it was too soon to arrest either of them. Apart from what he now knew about Eddie's financial troubles, all he had was Rose's information. As far as that was concerned, firstly he had to consider the possibility that she might have made a mistake. Secondly, if she was right about Heatherington being up to no good, he had a duty to protect her. He needed to be sure that a charge would stick, and that he wouldn't be forced to release the man. He reached for a piece of paper and in large letters wrote down three names: Eddie de Jong, Toby Heatherington, and Rupert Wilde. Then as an afterthought, he added Eddie's father Dickie. He was a less likely suspect than the others, but de Silva wasn't ready to discount him yet.

* * *

A call came from Archie as de Silva was eating the mid-morning snack of spicy dahl with shredded carrots which he'd sent Nadar to fetch from the bazaar after he'd briefed him and Prasanna on the telephone call with Inspector Singh.

'I'm glad I caught you, de Silva. My brother and his wife arrive this afternoon, so we'll be busy. Wanted to get this bit of information to you first.'

'No problem, sir.' De Silva wiped a speck of dahl from his lower lip. Even though Archie couldn't see him, formalities must be observed.

'The closest my contacts have managed to get is a fellow by the name of Thomas Heaton. He was stationed at Trincomalee, but he was moved on several months ago. There seems to be no information as to where he was posted, which seems odd. Someone suggested he might have been sent abroad. Of course, one has to bear in mind that there's a war on, and careless talk costs lives. From the description

I was given, Heaton and Heatherington might be the same person, but tall with curly brown hair could apply to a lot of young men. Pity Heatherington doesn't have any notably distinguishing features. Anything to report from your end?'

'I had a visit from Edmund Fallowfield.'

'Ah, I thought that might happen. I'm sorry. It sounds like I didn't do a very good job of warning him off. How did the meeting go?'

'As he did with you, he talked about the doping inquiry and was keen I should take a close look at Rupert Wilde. He suggested that Dickie de Jong might be involved in some way, but he didn't mention Eddie or his friend Toby. He also brought up Sunil's death.'

'I see. Anything else to tell me?'

De Silva explained what Inspector Singh had found out about Eddie.

'If he's having trouble placing bets, I would think doping his father's horses would do him no good,' said Archie. 'Equally, I can't see why Dickie de Jong would risk his reputation to make a bit more cash when he already stood to win the very substantial prize that comes with the Hill Country Cup. If there's anything in all of this, it seems to me the most likely answer is that our mystery man is Wilde. Interesting that Fallowfield is so keen on that theory,' he mused. 'What's your view of it?'

De Silva explained about the unfriendly exchange between the two men, and his idea of what might have been at the bottom of it.

'Alternatively,' said Archie when he had heard him out, 'Wilde may have cheated Fallowfield out of money. I know he's not been in Nuala long, but they might have been acquainted somewhere else. Of course, the other possibility is that Fallowfield does have a talent for sniffing out the truth and he's right about Wilde.' He chuckled. 'Don't worry, de Silva. You needn't retire just yet. Incidentally, I take it you managed to fob him off? We don't want him interfering.'

'I did my best, sir.'

'Good.' Archie cleared his throat. 'Well, time marches on. Our visitors will be here any minute, so I'll leave the problem in your capable hands.'

'Thank you, sir. Unless you have any objection, I think it may be time to speak to some of the members of the Jockey Club.'

There was a pause before Archie spoke. 'Very well, I leave that to your discretion.'

De Silva ended the call then propped his elbows on his desk and steepled his hands. He needed to think carefully about how to make his next move.

CHAPTER 15

He returned home for lunch and found Jane in the kitchen discussing the meals for the rest of the week with their cook.

'I didn't expect you back yet,' said Jane. 'I've told cook that I'll be satisfied with a few sandwiches for my lunch. I'm due to go to a meeting at the vicarage this afternoon to plan the Christmas flowers for the church. Florence has asked me to take over organising everything as she'll be busy with Archie's relations who are visiting them. I expect Mrs Peters will put on one of her famous teas after we've all had our discussion so if I have much for lunch beforehand, I shall probably burst.'

The cook looked at de Silva's face. 'I think I can make something that the sahib will like better than sandwiches,' he said.

'I'm glad to hear it.' De Silva gave him a grateful smile.

Half an hour later, as Jane ate her tomato sandwiches, he told her about his conversations with Singh and Archie and tucked into a generous plate of kottu roti, a dish he often had at the bazaar when he didn't come home for lunch, but made even more delicious when prepared by their cook, whose creamy scrambled eggs mixed beautifully with the chopped flatbreads, chillies, vegetables, and spices that made up the dish.

'Are you sure that will be enough for you?' asked Jane, raising an eyebrow.

De Silva chuckled. 'What are you implying? I have a very busy afternoon, so I need to be well fed beforehand.'

'What do you intend to do next?'

'I've sent Prasanna and Nadar up to the racecourse to make some more inquiries. I've given them the job of finding out if everyone who works up there has an alibi for the day of the Hill Country Cup, in particular that night when Sunil was killed. That should take care of Pat Masham and the clerk of the course, Peter Findley, amongst others. But I'll deal with Edmund Fallowfield myself. I must also talk to the de Jongs, Rupert Wilde, and Henry Fortescue, the chairman of the Jockey Club.'

'Won't that give it away that you think the circumstances of Sunil's death were suspicious?'

'Unfortunately, I don't think there's any other option now.'

'I suppose not, but will you speak to Archie first?'

'I already have done, and he agreed.'

'Good.' Jane ate the last bite of her sandwich. 'That was just right. Now, I'm sorry to leave you, but I think I'd better go and get ready.'

'How are you getting to the vicarage? Would you like me to drive you?'

'Thank you, dear, but it's out of your way and anyway, I have a lift.'

Left alone, de Silva speared a crunchy piece of cabbage with his fork and put it in his mouth. He wondered what kind of reception he would get at the Jockey Club. He knew the building: a rather grand one in the mould of the Crown Hotel, but he had never been inside it. He imagined that locals might encounter a certain amount of resistance.

'Let's hope my uniform solves that,' he remarked to Billy and Bella who had just joined him in the dining room.

The door opened and their servant Delisha came in. 'Cook asks if you would like anything more to eat, sahib.'

'No thank you. Please tell him the kottu was delicious as always.'

'Shall I clear away now, sahib?'

De Silva nodded then folded his napkin, pushed back his chair, and stood up. If he was lucky, Henry Fortescue and Rupert Wilde would be at the Jockey Club, but if not, he might at least be able to ascertain where he could find them.

* * *

At the Jockey Club, the forbidding black door with its snarling lion's head for a knocker was answered by a liveried flunky. De Silva gave his name and asked if Henry Fortescue or Rupert Wilde were available.

'Sahib Fortescue is not here today but Sahib Wilde is in the dining room having lunch. Shall I tell him you wish to see him?'

'Yes, please.'

De Silva stepped into a spacious if rather gloomy hall. The walls were panelled in dark wood, and black and white tiles covered the floor. A huge brass chandelier hung from the ceiling and the panelled wall opposite the front door was partly covered with a large tapestry. Its drab hues of brown, green and faded blue depicted a group of ladies and gentlemen in medieval costume riding through a forest. Several hard chairs with their top rails decorated with heraldic motifs lined the wall below.

A man wearing a dark suit and a self-important air hurried out from behind a desk. 'May I help you? I'm the manager here.'

'I understand Mr Rupert Wilde is in today. I'd like to see him,' said de Silva when he'd given his name.

'He's having lunch.'

'So your doorman said. I can wait.'

The manager glanced around the hall. De Silva presumed he was anxious no one saw that the police were visiting the club. 'Please come this way. I'll show you to one of our private rooms.'

De Silva followed him down a long corridor and into a small room papered with black-and-green-striped wallpaper. It smelled strongly of cigar smoke. The manager left him, and he sat down on one of the plum-coloured leather chairs.

Twenty minutes passed and he was beginning to wonder if Wilde would refuse to see him when he heard footsteps coming down the corridor. The door opened and Wilde walked in. De Silva noticed that his eyes looked a little unfocused. He didn't offer to shake hands but sat down abruptly on one of the other chairs. The smell of brandy reached de Silva's nose.

'Well, what did you want to see me about?' asked Wilde in a peremptory tone.

De Silva took out his notebook. 'I'd be obliged if you'd tell me what your movements were on the evening after the Hill Country Cup meeting.'

'What? Look, you'd better tell me what this is about. Am I being accused of something?'

'No, sir,' said de Silva patiently. *Although you may be eventually*, he thought to himself. 'But we have reason to believe that Sunil, the young man who worked at the stables and was found dead the morning after the meeting, didn't die accidentally. We're asking everyone who has a connection to the course or the stables to explain their whereabouts as a means of elimination. I'm aware of your connection to the racecourse through this club and I understand you also keep a horse at the stables.'

Wilde leaned forward in his chair. The smell of brandy intensified; de Silva saw that where his thick dark hair sprang from his forehead, it was damp with sweat. 'What makes you think that this fellow Sunil was murdered?'

'It may be that the test results for Garnet and Bright Star were incorrect. If so, Sunil may have witnessed someone tampering with the horses before the Hill Country Cup.'

'Incorrect?' snorted Wilde. 'That's nonsense. The tests are widely accepted and you've no business questioning the validity of the Jockey Club's decision. If you're right about this lad being murdered, you ought to be talking to the people he worked with, or his neighbours. Most likely there was some kind of trouble between them, and he came off worst. These locals are a rough lot.'

De Silva ignored the slur. He noticed that Wilde didn't express any concern over Sunil's possible fate.

'Nevertheless, I'd be obliged if you'd answer my question.'

Wilde grunted. 'Oh, very well. I suppose there's no harm in telling you where I was. After the meeting ended, I went back to my bungalow to bathe and change. If you want that corroborating, my servants can oblige. I spent the rest of the evening at the Residence. The party broke up around midnight and I returned home and went to bed.'

'Can you recall who you spoke to at the party?' he asked.

'I know a lot of people in Nuala, Inspector,' snapped Wilde. 'Do you really expect me to remember the details of every conversation?'

'I understand. May I ask what time you went up to the course on the day of the meeting?'

'It must have been about eleven o'clock. Various people including Pat Masham saw me and can vouch for that. I went to visit my horse Sultan then there were drinks and lunch in the clubroom.'

'And before you went to the stables?'

'I was at home. You can ask the servants if you want.'

'Did you spend time at the stables in the days running up to the meeting?'

'I came up a couple of times to exercise Sultan.'

'Did you happen to notice anyone you didn't recognise?'

'No,' said Wilde flatly. 'Anything else you'd like to know?'

'Not at the moment. Thank you for your help. Do you know where I might find Henry Fortescue?'

'This afternoon? No idea. He may be at his plantation. They can give you the address at the desk, but I've no doubt he'll give you short shrift too.'

De Silva put away his notebook. 'I'll have a word with them. Thank you again for your time.'

CHAPTER 16

Henry Fortescue's plantation was five miles to the north of town. A quick telephone call established that he was available. The drive out helped to dispel de Silva's irritation. Rupert Wilde was no more objectionable than many of the Britishers he had come across in his career. He had often wondered if they would conduct themselves in a similar way in their own country, or whether living in someone else's made them feel they had the right to behave however they chose to.

The private drive leading to the plantation was intimidating in its grandeur, lined with fine trees and in better condition than some country roads. Eventually the plantation came into sight. Its large, imposing main house was surrounded by extensive gardens that were dotted with smaller buildings including a Roman ruin and a Gothic folly.

De Silva had been told he was likely to find Fortescue down at his factory, so he took a left turn where the drive divided, bringing into view a clutch of long, low corrugated-iron buildings at the bottom of a gentle slope. Several empty carts were drawn up in the deserted yard and four grey mules drowsed in the shade of a persimmon tree. He parked the car and went over to the entrance to the largest building. As he drew close, he smelled tea and heard the hum of voices and machinery. A plantation's workplaces were always dusty. He wished he'd brought something to put over his mouth so that he didn't inhale the dust, but luckily Fortescue met him before he'd gone much further and suggested they talk in his office. To de Silva's mild surprise, it was a spartan room with buff-coloured walls. Two metal filing cabinets spewed paperwork, and shelves held files and a collection of breeding and racing yearbooks that looked well thumbed. Fortescue gestured to a chair. 'Take a pew, Inspector.'

'Thank you.'

Fortescue sat down behind his desk. 'Now then, I've already had a call from Wilde so no need to beat about the bush. I understand you're claiming that our inquiry into Garnet and Bright Star is invalid.'

'I believe that may be the case, sir.'

'Let me make it absolutely clear that the Jockey Club resists any insinuations that the affair was dealt with improperly. I suggest you think very carefully before you persist in your allegations.'

'I'm sure your verdict was reached in good faith, sir,' said de Silva quickly. 'But I understand that the tests aren't completely reliable.'

'What's your authority for that?'

'The government veterinary adviser, George Appleby.'

'Appleby's entitled to his opinion, but I disagree. The committee considered the matter thoroughly and were satisfied there was no wrongdoing. As for the death of this stable lad that you mentioned to Wilde, I suggest as he did that if you believe he was murdered, you look closer to home for the culprit.'

De Silva gritted his teeth. Obviously, he wasn't going to receive any more sympathetic a hearing from Fortescue than he had from Wilde. He pulled out his notebook. 'For the record, I'd be grateful if you'd tell me what your movements were after the race meeting.'

Fortescue scowled. 'This is a waste of my time, but very well.' He proceeded to give a detailed account of his evening and the people he had spoken to at the Clutterbucks' party. 'Is that enough for you?' he finished with a touch of sarcasm in his voice.

'Yes, thank you.'

'Good. One of the servants will see you out.' Fortescue didn't stand up and by the time de Silva reached the study door, he had returned to his paperwork.

* * *

The sun was already low in the sky as de Silva drove away from the plantation. He was angry about Fortescue's behaviour but then what had he expected, he asked himself. Darkness fell before he reached town. Away from Nuala's lights, the sky was an inky black peppered with the brightest of stars. It was a beautiful sight, and slowly he felt his anger subside.

It wasn't long before he saw the glow of the town ahead. When he arrived at Sunnybank, he found Jane in the hall, still in her outdoor clothes.

'Another meeting?' he asked.

She made a face. 'You wouldn't believe how complicated it is deciding who's to be responsible for what. One would think Christmas had never happened before. I'm beginning to have more admiration than I used to do for Florence and her way of managing things.'

'I never thought I'd hear you say that.'

Jane laughed. 'I've rather surprised myself. Now, enough of committees. Tell me about your afternoon. Did you manage to speak to everyone you wanted?'

'Rupert Wilde was at the Jockey Club, and I drove over to see Henry Fortescue at his plantation.' He proceeded to tell her about his conversations with the two men. 'I don't have much hope of any cooperation from either of them,' he finished.

'Do you think Wilde's supporting the club's decision in order to cover his tracks?'

'I'm not sure. Of course, if he's guilty, the last thing he would want is for the decision to be thrown into doubt.'

With Billy following her, Bella appeared in the hall. De Silva bent down to stroke them. 'Hello, you two. I hope you've not been getting into too much trouble today.' He straightened up and rolled his shoulders to ease them. 'Do we have long before dinner?'

'About an hour. But if you're very hungry, I'll ask cook to serve it a little earlier.'

'No need for that. I'm happy to sit on the verandah for a while with a whisky. Will you join me?'

'I have one or two things to do then I'll come out.'

'I'll have your sherry ready for you.'

Jane smiled. 'Thank you.'

In the drawing room he poured their drinks and took them out to the verandah. After the sultry heat of the day, the temperature was perfect. He relaxed into his chair and sipped his whisky, listening to the soothing throb of insects and the rustle of leaves stirred by a gentle breeze. It would be an hour before the moon rose, so the garden was a pool of darkness enclosed by the looming silhouettes of trees. He breathed in the scents that wafted towards him.

Jane emerged from the bungalow and sat down in the wicker chair beside his. 'Emerald gave me a lift home from the meeting,' she remarked. 'She asked after you and sent her good wishes.'

'That was kind of her.'

'I felt rather guilty that she has to come out of her way though. She always says she doesn't mind but I know she wanted to get home to see Olivia before their ayah put her to bed.'

De Silva glanced at her sideways. He wondered what was coming next.

Jane's face took on its determined expression. 'I've been thinking about it for quite a while; I've decided it's time I learned to drive. After all, more and more women do now. Why, if they're engaged in war work, they drive all sorts of vehicles – ambulances, trucks, tractors.'

A wave of trepidation washed over de Silva. He liked to think of himself as a man who was reasonably modern in his outlook, but a learner driver, even one as sensible as Jane, in charge of his beloved Morris was too daunting a prospect for him to cope with. And what if she expected him to teach her? It might stretch marital harmony to breaking point.

Jane laughed. 'Oh, don't look so worried. I wouldn't dream of asking you to let me learn in the Morris.'

'Then what would you do?' De Silva was puzzled.

'Do you remember the legacy my Aunt Margaret left me? I've never spent it, so I might use it to buy myself a little car. I'll need some help deciding what to get of course, but perhaps we could look for one together, and Jayasena is happy to give me lessons.' She paused. 'Shanti?'

'This is all rather sudden,' he said cautiously.

'But you wouldn't mind, would you?'

There was a long pause then he smiled. 'I suppose I know when I'm beaten.'

Reaching across, Jane gave him a sharp tap on the arm. He chuckled. 'No, of course I don't mind. You go ahead. I'm sure you'll be an excellent driver.' He was glad too that Jayasena would be teaching her. He was a reliable man and hopefully a new activity would provide some distraction from his family's tragic loss.

Jane smiled. 'Thank you, Shanti. I'm glad that's settled.'

They chatted about what car she might buy until they went inside for dinner. The subject of the case didn't come up again, but later, as he took a walk around the garden by the light of the newly risen moon, de Silva's mind returned to it. If anything, it was more puzzling now than it had been at the outset. Rose Appleby's information suggested that Toby Heatherington, perhaps in league with Eddie de Jong, might be the villain. But then Edmund Fallowfield had brought Rupert Wilde into the picture. Perhaps he shouldn't rule out Henry Fortescue either. His alibi appeared to be sound, and he was probably denying everything to support the club's decision, but it was conceivable there was more to it, and if so, he might have employed someone else to do his dirty work and silence poor Sunil.

He stopped by one of his roses and drank in the perfume, noticing that some of the plant's glossy leaves had a few tiny holes in them. Presumably, caterpillars had made them. Carefully, he turned over the damaged leaves to see if any were still there but there was no sign of them. Perhaps they had already turned into moths or butterflies. It was sad to think that after that, their lives and the beauty they brought to the world would be so brief; in most cases only a few weeks before they died. In the scale of human life, Sunil's time on earth had been almost as short, but it was man, not nature, that had brought about its premature end. De Silva's jaw tightened. Whoever was responsible, he was determined to make sure that they paid for their crime.

He wondered how Prasanna and Nadar had got on at the stables. He was proud of the way that over the years they had both grown in confidence and ability. He had almost suggested that they should speak to Edmund Fallowfield as well as the rest of the people who worked at the stables, but then decided against it. He might be wrong, but he had the feeling that Fallowfield was the kind of man who would have definite ideas about the respect that was due to him. He might be offended by a visit from junior officers and that would make it particularly hard to question him. The same would almost certainly apply to Dickie de Jong, and if he interviewed the man, it would be natural and convenient to talk to Eddie and his friend Toby at the same time. He turned back towards the bungalow. Tomorrow was going to be another busy day. Hopefully when it was over, he would be able to understand things more clearly.

CHAPTER 17

Before Jane was dressed, de Silva breakfasted alone then drove up to the racecourse. It was busy at the livery stables. The horses that were kept there were being taken out for their morning exercise whilst the day was still cool. Edmund Fallowfield hadn't been in his office when de Silva passed by, but he saw Pat Masham emerge from one of the looseboxes, so he went over to talk to him.

Masham gave him a shrewd look. 'I wondered when you'd turn up. A couple of your boys were here yesterday asking questions. They didn't give much away but something's up, isn't it? I'd like to know what.'

'I'm afraid I have reason to believe that the circumstances surrounding your stable lad Sunil's death are suspicious.'

'Surely it was an accident. What makes you think he was killed?'

'There may be a connection to the allegations of doping in the Hill Country Cup.'

Masham paused a moment, his brow furrowing. 'Are you saying the inquiry might have come up with the wrong answer? The Jockey Club aren't going to like that. You'd better be very sure of your ground. I hope none of my lads are suspects. They're a good lot and they were always kind to Sunil. If you're going to try and put the finger on any of them, I'll tell you for nothing you're barking up the wrong tree.'

'Thank you.' De Silva gave him a dry smile.

'So, who's in the frame?'

'Whilst my inquiries are in progress, I'm not able to tell you that.'

Masham scowled. De Silva wondered if he was going to be difficult but then he shrugged. 'I had to give it a try, didn't I?'

There was a penetrating squeak, and a stable lad came out of one of the barns wheeling a barrow. De Silva smelled the pungent odour of manure. Masham cupped a hand to his mouth. 'Get that ruddy thing oiled,' he shouted irritably.

'Yes, sahib.'

Masham turned back to de Silva. 'If it's not one thing it's another. This place used to run like clockwork and would still if I was left alone to do things my way.' His eyes narrowed. 'I've always had the Jockey Club lot breathing down my neck, but at least they have the justification of owning the course and the livery side of it, but now Fallowfield's come along into the bargain, acting as if he knows all there is to know about the business.'

'Actually, it was Mr Fallowfield that I was hoping to have a word with but he's not in his office. Do you have any idea where I might find him?'

'He might be up here later but if you want him in a hurry, you could try him at home.' He made the gesture of writing in the air. 'Got a pen? I'll give you the address.'

De Silva pulled out his notebook. 'Fire away.' He jotted down the address then closed the book. 'Thank you.'

'Hasn't been here long as you may know,' said Masham. 'And I can't tell you much about him, except he mentioned something about working in India before he came to Ceylon, or maybe it was Malaya.'

'How does he get on with the staff?'

'Doesn't take much notice of them to be honest. I'd be surprised if he knows all their names.'

'What about Sunil?'

'I'd say the same.'

'And the committee members of the Jockey Club?'

Masham grinned sourly. 'I've never heard them complain but then he knows how to butter up the toffs.'

So, in Masham's opinion, Fallowfield was a snob, thought de Silva. He thanked him for his help and went back to the Morris. He would have to pass the police station anyway to get to the address Masham had given him so he might as well stop off and telephone ahead. If Fallowfield was out, it would save him a journey.

At the station, Prasanna and Nadar were both in the public room, Prasanna diligently studying a thick file and Nadar typing a report on the station's elderly Remington typewriter. His typing still left something to be desired, its rhythm and pace bringing to de Silva's mind the image of an old crow hopping from stepping-stone to stepping-stone across a pond.

With a scrape of chairs, both young men stood up. 'Good morning, sir.'

'As you were, I'm not staying long. I've just been up to the stables. Pat Masham quizzed me about what you were doing yesterday. Well done for keeping your counsel, but I decided to tell him there's evidence that Sunil's death wasn't an accident.'

'How did he take it, sir?' asked Prasanna.

'He was sceptical and quick to defend his staff.'

He proceeded to give them the gist of his conversations with Rupert Wilde and Henry Fortescue. 'Wilde may have been covering something up,' he added, 'as might Henry Fortescue unless they were just running true to type. Now, I want to speak to Edmund Fallowfield and Masham suggested I try him at home.' He took out his notebook and handed it to Nadar. 'Here's the number. Call him for me, please. If he's in, I'll take the call in my office.'

He hadn't long sat down at his desk when the telephone

rang, and Nadar's voice came on the line. 'I'm sorry, sir, the telephone lines in that area are out of order. The exchange can't tell me when they'll be back. They think that elephants may have knocked down some of the poles last night.'

'Ah.' De Silva imagined a herd of elephants, angry at the invasion of their ancestral lands by the forces of civilisation, although it was probably just that they'd fancied using the telegraph poles as scratching posts. He might as well drive out there on the off chance.

* * *

As he drove through town, de Silva noticed the Residence's official car cruising in the opposite direction, its chauffeur ramrod straight at the wheel in his white uniform and red turban. In the back were two ladies, one of them Florence. He presumed the other was the troublesome sister-in-law. Archie and his brother must be otherwise occupied, perhaps with a game of golf or some fishing. But the sight reminded him that he ought not to leave his boss out of the picture for too long. He had a feeling there were going to be complaints from Fortescue and Wilde. Archie would be far more likely to take them in his stride if he'd had a chance to prepare himself.

Fallowfield's bungalow was situated in one of the less attractive parts of town. The garden around the property looked dry and dusty. Clearly, he wasn't a fan of gardening. De Silva parked to one side of the bungalow where there was a patch of land with a few outbuildings along the back of it, walked around to the front door and was just reaching for the knocker when the door opened, and a servant looked out. De Silva asked for Fallowfield and was soon shown to his study. It was very different from Archie Clutterbuck's comfortable one. That was furnished with mellow furniture, antique rugs, shelves of leather-bound books, silver-framed photographs, and pieces of sporting memorabilia. This room was clean and neat but impersonal.

'Inspector de Silva!' Fallowfield stood up from his desk to greet him. 'I certainly didn't expect to see you here. To what do I owe the pleasure?'

'I'm sorry to take you unawares, sir. I tried to telephone but I understand that the line is out of order.'

'Yes, unfortunately it is. How did you know I'd be here?'

'I went up to the racecourse. Pat Masham suggested you might be at home.'

'So, what can I do for you?'

'I have a few questions.'

Fallowfield sat down again and motioned to the opposite chair. 'Well, what do you want to ask me?'

'We have reason to believe that the stable lad Sunil's death wasn't accidental, and in view of that, I need to build up a picture of the whereabouts of everyone involved with the racecourse and its stables on the day of his death. I'd be obliged if you would tell me where you were, beginning with the morning of the race meeting.'

'Considering that you and your boss were less than keen to afford me a hearing on previous occasions about the criminal activity that may have been going on at the racecourse, there's a certain irony to this, Inspector. But of course murder is a serious business and I'm very concerned to hear that you suspect one has taken place. May I ask what evidence prompted your change of heart?'

'I believe there may be a connection to the alleged doping of Garnet and Bright Star before the Hill Country Cup.'

'Hmm, interesting that you're coming around to my way of thinking. Naturally, I'm happy to help with your inquiries in any way I can. Let me see. I breakfasted here early. Afterwards I went straight up to the course. Race days are always busy and there were a hundred and one matters that needed my attention. Once the meeting started, I also had a lot to do and barely had a moment alone. If you wish, I can give you the names of people who will vouch for my activities.' He gave de Silva a dry smile. 'Of course one of them would be yourself.'

'Thank you, I'll let you know if I need names. What about after the meeting?'

'I went home. I'd received an invitation to the party at the Residence, but I was too tired to attend. I'm afraid I'm not a very sociable creature at the best of times.'

'On the day of the race meeting or in the week leading up to it, did you notice anyone you didn't recognise at the stables?'

Fallowfield leaned back in his chair. He seemed deep in thought. 'No,' he said at last. 'Should I have done? Do you have anyone in particular in mind?'

De Silva shook his head. 'It's merely a routine question.'

'Look, I've told you my suspicions about Wilde, Inspector. With respect, in my opinion your time would be better spent pursuing him, not asking routine questions.'

'I assure you I have no intention of neglecting any avenues of investigation.'

'Good. Maybe Rose Appleby could shed some light on the subject. I believe she was close to the deceased.'

'Naturally I'll be speaking to her.' De Silva quietly forgave himself for his economy with the truth.

'A charming young lady, Rose Appleby, and an excellent rider. I'm sure she could match herself against many men. I hope the members of the Jockey Club will be impressed by the popularity of the ladies' race and agree to include more of them in the calendar.'

He stood up. 'Forgive me for hurrying you, Inspector, but if there's nothing else, I have a good deal to be getting on with. If you feel able to share information with me from now on, I'll be very interested to hear how your inquiries progress.'

Privately reflecting that was unlikely, de Silva thanked him and Fallowfield showed him out. On the way back to the Morris, he passed a lean-to garage that he'd noticed on the way in. There were two cars parked there, both 1920s classics. A servant with a sponge and a bucket of soapy water was busy washing the one at the front. De Silva went over to have a better look and the man paused in his task. 'Can I help you, sahib?'

'I'm interested in these.' De Silva pointed to the cars. 'One doesn't often see such fine examples of the era. Does your master drive them much?'

The servant smiled. 'Not often, but they are always kept clean.'

'Very laudable.' De Silva circled the front car, admiring its elegant lines and gleaming chrome and paintwork, then turned his attention to the one behind it. It was when he walked around the back of it that he noticed some rags in the corner of the garage. They were stained with something that might have been blood. He was about to go closer for a better look when he heard a voice. He looked up and saw that Fallowfield had joined them in the garage. 'Still here?' he asked.

'I was admiring your very fine cars.'

'I'm glad you approve. Cars are something of a hobby of mine.'

'Did you buy them in Ceylon?'

'Only one of them. The other one was shipped from America.'

An expensive business, thought de Silva. Perhaps his initial impression that Fallowfield was not particularly well off had been mistaken.

Fallowfield smiled. 'I imagine you're wondering how a humble secretary affords such things. I was fortunate enough to inherit some money from a distant relative. I suppose many people would have done something more prudent with it, but I have no dependants, which leaves me free to do as I like.'

He nodded to his servant who waited with the dripping sponge in his hand. 'Carry on.'

'Yes, sahib.'

De Silva cast a last glance at the bundle of rags. On second thoughts, the marks on them might have been made by oil or dirt, but it was a pity there was no way of taking a better look without arousing Fallowfield's suspicion. Perhaps he could find a discreet way of coming back another time.

CHAPTER 18

After he left Edmund Fallowfield, de Silva decided to go straight to the de Jongs' estate. The afternoon was already half over, and he preferred to make journeys out of town during daylight. He stopped briefly, however, at a roadside stall to buy a bowl of noodles with chopped spiced vegetables.

As he ate, he thought about how to approach the task ahead of him. He must be prepared for Dickie de Jong being a difficult man to question, even if in a less overt way than Rupert Wilde had been. Wilde was openly aggressive, but de Silva suspected that behind Dickie's air of bonhomie, there was a shrewd character who would be adept at hiding anything that he didn't want to reveal. He thought of Fallowfield's remarks about Dickie's attitude to money. If it was correct that he had very little of his own and had to rely on his wife to support his expensive lifestyle, it wasn't hard to imagine that he would eventually find the situation humiliating and try to devise a way out. Or perhaps Grace de Jong had threatened to ration her contributions or end them altogether. In either case, Dickie might have resorted to desperate measures to get money.

He scraped up the last of the noodles and ate them. A delicious savoury smell wafted from the steaming pans on the stall and for a moment he was tempted to buy another bowl, but the sun would be going down in less than two hours. Safety over appetite was a good maxim.

The road became rougher and loose stones skittered away under the Morris's wheels. Despite de Silva's efforts to avoid potholes, on the narrower sections of road it was a choice between driving too close to the edge and the steep descent into the valley or bumping over them. He guessed that he was still several miles from the plantation when he heard the roar of an engine. A car was approaching at such a speed that he was forced to wrench the steering wheel sideways to get out of its way. As it flashed past, he saw the driver in profile and thought he recognised Eddie de Jong. His heart thumping, he righted the Morris and brought her to a halt. When he looked over his shoulder, the other car was already out of sight. He didn't want to think about how close he had come to the edge of the road and the steep drop, but it was hard not to. A few moments passed before he was ready to drive again.

A mile further on, he felt a tug on the steering wheel and then a series of bone-shaking jolts. Irritably, he brought the Morris to a halt and got out to inspect the damage. One of the front tyres was flat.

'Drat!' he muttered. There was little chance of help up here on this unfrequented road. He'd have to change it himself. He took off his jacket and threw it on the passenger seat then rolled up his sleeves and found his toolbox. It didn't take him long to remove the spare from the back of the Morris but jacking the car up and changing the wheel was a longer and considerably more arduous job.

By the time he'd finished, his shirt was sticking to his back. He winced as he hauled himself to his feet. His hands were black with oily grime, so he cleaned himself up as best as he could with his handkerchief then stuffed it in the glove compartment. Before he got back into the Morris, he stopped to admire the sky; it was a blaze of crimson and gold scattered with indigo clouds. He supposed the sight was some recompense for his exertions. It was unfortunate, however, that now he would be lucky to reach the de Jongs' place in the light, let alone get back to Nuala.

He drove on more slowly than before, the beams of the Morris's headlights picking out the road as darkness swiftly enveloped the countryside around him. A nagging worry crept in that he was on the wrong road but then with a wave of relief, he saw lights up ahead. It must be the de Jongs' house.

* * *

It was an imposing place, painted white with a central section rising to two storeys, flanked by lower wings. There were lights in the windows of the one to de Silva's left, and an open-topped Jaguar and a white Rolls Royce were parked on the drive. It looked as if someone was at home; a relief after the unnerving journey. If it had been Eddie he'd seen in the speeding car, he might be able to find him later in town.

He went up to the front door and rang the bell. Whilst he waited for it to be answered, he was surprised to see that the paint on the windows to either side of the door was flaking, exposing dry wood underneath. The windowsills were also in need of redecoration. The porch was floored with beautiful blue and white tiles that looked antique but several of them were cracked.

The door opened and a servant peered out. He seemed taken aback at the sight of de Silva and greeted him nervously. 'Are your master and mistress in?' de Silva asked. The servant mumbled an assent.

'I'm Inspector de Silva of the Nuala police. Please tell them I'd be grateful for a few minutes of their time.'

'The memsahib is sick and resting, but I will ask the sahib.'

De Silva took a step into the hall. 'Please do so. I'll wait here.'

The servant hurried away, and de Silva looked around the hall. It was large and square, lit by two huge brass chandeliers of intricate design. The walls were panelled with oak stained a deep brown and the floor was made of black and white tiles. A long, narrow table with legs that had the girth of small tree trunks stood against the wall opposite the door. On it was a display of blue and white Delftware jugs and bowls. There were also ornate chairs with high backs and cane seats, and on the walls, portraits with the sitters dressed in silks and satins. Their stiff poses and solemn faces suggested that they hadn't enjoyed the experience but had presumably submitted to it in the interest of showing the world their wealth and importance.

'Please come this way, sahib.' The servant had reappeared and soon de Silva was following him through several elegant but slightly shabby rooms, eventually arriving at a dimly lit one that was smaller than the others and more simply furnished with a few small tables, a wall of bookshelves, and several armchairs upholstered in olive-green leather.

Dickie de Jong didn't get up from the one he sat in. He looked dishevelled, his pale linen jacket and trousers crumpled, and the top three buttons of his white shirt undone, revealing the grey hairs on his chest. He ran a hand through his black hair – too black to be convincing, thought de Silva – and wearily pushed it away from his forehead. There was a lamp and an empty glass on the table beside him.

'Good evening, Inspector. You've come a long way. I can't imagine what for, but I'll do my best to help. I'm afraid my wife is indisposed, and my son has gone into town, so I'll have to do.' He indicated the empty glass at his elbow. 'Drinking alone is a dispiriting occupation. Will you have a whisky with me?'

'Thank you, but I'm afraid I'm on duty.'

Dickie rolled his eyes. 'A concept with which, as my wife will tell you, I'm unfamiliar.' There was bitterness in his voice. De Silva presumed that Grace de Jong's indisposition might have more to do with a recent quarrel with her husband than an illness.

'If you've no objection, I'll think I'll have one.'

'Of course not.'

The servant who had shown de Silva in was still hovering by the door. Dickie raised his glass, and the cut crystal caught the light from the table lamp. 'Another one, Selim. No soda.'

Selim hesitated and Dickie folded his arms across his chest. 'Are you deaf?'

'I'm sorry, sahib, but the memsahib—'

'To hell with that. The memsahib isn't here, is she? Now do as I tell you.'

'Very well, sahib,' Selim said unhappily. He took the glass and left the room.

'Shall we get to the point, Inspector? If this is about the inquiry regarding the Hill Country Cup, I don't think I have anything to add to what I told Fortescue and his chaps, and they were satisfied there was no impropriety.'

'So I understand, sir. I am, however, asking everyone with any connection to the race for a detailed account of their movements that day.'

'Why?'

'Because one of the stable lads was later found dead in suspicious circumstances.'

'I'm sorry to hear it.' Dickie paused. 'I hope you're not suggesting that it was connected to the inquiry in any way.'

'At this stage nothing can be ruled out. It's a known fact that the available tests are not entirely reliable.'

Dickie bridled. 'I take strong exception to that, as I'm sure the Jockey Club would. And if you're implying that

I had something to do with this stable lad's death, you're wrong. Who was he anyway?'

'His name was Sunil.'

'Sunil, do you say? I remember him. The Applebys' daughter Rose was very fond of him. I believe he grew up in their household. He was excellent with horses. I talked with him sometimes when I came up to the stables. Poor fellow. Are you sure it wasn't an accident? How did he die?'

'He was found in one of the barns at the stables with a broken neck.'

'Could he have fallen from somewhere? There are hay-lofts that are quite a height in those barns.'

'Nothing's certain at present, sir. I'm making my inquiries to build up as clear a picture as possible of what happened that day.'

'Despite the successful outcome of the race, I have to admit it's one that I'd largely prefer to forget,' said Dickie, mellowing a little. 'But ask away, Inspector.'

As de Silva took out his notebook, he heard the sound of a telephone ringing. It stopped and he wondered if Selim or one of the other servants would come to fetch Dickie, but when a few moments had passed and they were still alone, he went back to concentrating on the questions he wanted to ask. He was interested to find that despite the state he was in, Dickie seemed to have considerably better powers of recall than Rupert Wilde. Ten minutes later, he had given a creditably full account of the day of the Hill Country Cup from early morning to its close after Florence's party at the Residence.

De Silva thanked him and put his notebook away. 'I'd hoped to speak to your son and his friend Toby Heatherington,' he said. 'Do you know where I can find them?'

'As I said, Eddie left just before you arrived. You might find him in the bar at the Crown. It seems my whisky isn't good enough for him. As for Heatherington, he left yesterday. Said he had business to see to in Kandy. My son might know where he's to be found.'

He got up. 'I'll see you to the door. I'd like to know where that ruddy whisky's got to.'

De Silva followed him back through the rooms that led to the hall. They had reached the final one when he heard a man and a woman talking. In the hall were Grace de Jong and the servant Selim. Grace swung around to face her husband. Her face was as pale as her dress. 'There's been a call from the Crown,' she said. 'It's Eddie. He's had an accident.'

CHAPTER 19

At the Crown, a car was being towed away that de Silva recognised as the one that had almost run him off the road on his way up to the de Jongs' estate. Its front end was a crumpled mess. There was no sign of another vehicle.

De Silva, Dickie, and Grace hurried up the stairs into the reception area and Dickie went up to the desk. 'Where's my son?' he barked at the startled receptionist.

'We're looking for Eddie de Jong,' said de Silva, joining him.

The receptionist reached for the telephone. 'I'll call the manager, sir. He's expecting you.'

A few moments later, de Silva's friend Sanjeewa Gunesekera arrived and introduced himself. He ushered them through to a quiet lounge where they found Eddie. Grace rushed over to him and put her arms around him. 'Are you alright?'

He brushed her off. 'Yes,' he said curtly.

A hurt look came over her face.

'Don't speak to your mother like that,' snapped Dickie. 'What's been going on?'

Eddie looked belligerent and didn't speak. Sanjeewa stepped forward. 'If I may, I'll explain.'

'I'm glad someone has a tongue in their head,' Dickie said testily.

'Mr Wilde was due to dine here. The doorman on duty

tells me that he was just arriving in his car when your son drove up behind him. The doorman was surprised that he was going as fast as he was. A moment later he drove into the back of Mr Wilde's car.'

'Where's the car now? I saw only my son's damaged one outside.'

'As it could still be driven, it has already been moved out of sight, but unfortunately, Mr Wilde was thrown forward by the impact and hit his head on the windscreen. Doctor Hebden has been called and is with him now.'

Grace looked dismayed. 'Oh, Eddie, what have you done?'

'You ask me that?'

She turned away from him, her lips set in a thin line.

Dickie suddenly took charge. 'What do you want us to do, Inspector?' he asked briskly. 'My wife and I would like to take our son home. Do you require a surety of some kind that he won't try to leave before this is all sorted out? I assure you that we'll make sure he stays put. No other car will be put at his disposal. As you've seen, his own will need extensive repair before it can be driven again. If it's acceptable to you, we'd be grateful if questioning him could wait until the morning.'

De Silva deliberated for a moment. It was irregular but in Eddie's present mood, it seemed unlikely he would get much out of him in any case. 'I'm happy to accept your assurance,' he said at last. 'But I'll want to interview him first thing tomorrow.'

'Thank you,' Grace said quietly.

'How serious are Wilde's injuries?' asked Dickie.

'Doctor Hebden thinks the concussion may only be mild,' said Sanjeewa, 'But he wants to keep him under observation overnight before deciding whether it's safe to let him go home.'

'May we see him?'

'I'll ask Doctor Hebden. If Mr Wilde agrees, I imagine he won't object.'

'Will you deal with that, Dickie?' asked Grace. 'I'd like to take Eddie home.' She held out her hand to her son. 'Come, my dear. Mr Sanjeewa, would you be so kind as to call us a taxi?'

'Of course, ma'am.'

'We'll wait here.'

'I'll go and arrange it and speak to the doctor.'

When he was left alone with the de Jongs, that British expression came into de Silva's mind: one could have cut the silence with a knife. In this case, he thought, it would need to be a very large meat cleaver. There was a palpable air of relief in the room when Sanjeewa returned to say that a taxi awaited Grace and Eddie, and Doctor Hebden agreed to de Silva and Dickie seeing Rupert Wilde.

* * *

Wilde had been put in a bedroom on a corridor well away from the main area of the hotel. Sanjeewa knocked on the door and de Silva heard David Hebden's voice telling them to enter. Propped up on a mound of pillows, Wilde had his head swathed in a large white bandage. His eyes were heavy lidded, and he didn't utter a greeting.

'It looks like Mr Wilde has been lucky,' said Hebden when Dickie de Jong had introduced himself. 'Although to be on the safe side, I'd like to keep an eye on him for another day or two.'

Dickie went over to Wilde's bedside. His usual jaunty manner had been replaced by a sombre air. 'I'm very sorry about this. My son can be hot-blooded at times.'

De Silva was surprised that Wilde didn't seem angry. There appeared to be something between the two men that he didn't understand.

Wilde turned his attention from Dickie to de Silva. 'I won't be pressing charges,' he said. 'I think the whole affair is best forgotten.'

A profound look of relief crossed Dickie's face.

'It was a misunderstanding,' Wilde went on.

This was becoming curiouser and curiouser, thought de Silva. What had happened to the fiery, antagonistic character he had met previously? Perhaps the knock on the head had occasioned a change for the better.

'I take it you have no objection to leaving the matter there, Inspector,' Wilde added with a hint of his former domineering tone.

'If you're sure that's what you want, sir.' De Silva turned to Dickie. 'I still need to speak to your son. I'll want his assurance that there will be no repetition of this incident. He must also understand that if there are any more breaches of the peace, severe penalties will follow.'

Dickie nodded. 'I'll make sure he does, Inspector.' He looked over at Wilde. 'Please send the bill for repairing your car to me. And yours, Doctor Hebden,' he added.

'Well,' said Hebden. 'If there's nothing more to discuss, I'd like my patient to get some rest. I'll arrange for one of my nurses to come to the hotel in case you need anything, Mr Wilde, and I'll be on call if required.'

Wilde thanked him. De Silva took a last look as he followed Hebden and Dickie out of the room. Wilde's eyes were already closed.

* * *

'So, what do you make of that, de Silva?' asked Hebden when they'd said goodbye to Dickie de Jong and were on their way to have a word with Sanjeewa and bring him up to date. 'From what I've heard of Rupert Wilde, his behaviour's hardly what I would have expected. Even allowing for the fact that he's unlikely to be feeling at his best.'

'I agree I was surprised. Do you think he'll make a full recovery?'

'I'm confident of it, but after an accident like that, one never wants to give the patient the idea that they can return to normal immediately. A rest will do Wilde no harm, even if it's not strictly necessary.' He frowned. 'I wonder why he was so conciliatory. Something to hide, do you think?' He gave de Silva a quizzical look. 'Might there be something you'd like to tell me?'

De Silva hesitated. It wasn't really proper for him to share inside information about an investigation with third parties, but with David Hebden, it was rather a different situation. He had been privy to police matters before and his discretion could be relied upon. He gave Hebden an outline of the case so far, concluding it with his last conversation with Edmund Fallowfield. 'Perhaps there's something in Fallowfield's theory about Wilde,' he went on. 'But after this incident, it occurs to me that rather than being the only villain, Wilde may be in league with Eddie de Jong. If they fell out, Eddie might have lost his temper and caused the crash.'

'It would be a foolish thing to do. Anyway, would Eddie de Jong really get involved in doping his own parents' horses?'

'He has reason to be bitter about his father and apparently he's also in financial trouble.'

'Hmm, and the outsider winning could have made him a lot of money.'

'It's most likely an accomplice would have placed the bet. I understand Eddie's credit is no longer good with the bookies.'

'So that's where Wilde would come in, eh?'

'As none of the bookies we've spoken to recognised

Wilde's description, a third party seems more probable. I'm interested to hear whether all this changes your diagnosis of the cause of Sunil's death.'

'I still think it's plausible that he fell and broke his neck, but on the other hand it's not beyond the bounds of possibility that the injury was deliberate. To break a man's neck, an attacker would need to be strong and know what they were doing, but it can be done, especially if they have the element of surprise in their favour.'

'Hmm, so let's say Sunil wasn't expecting to be attacked. He was slight in build and from what I've heard, a gentle creature, so unlikely to fight back.'

They had reached Sanjeewa's office. 'How much are you going to tell him?' asked Hebden. 'If he knows anything about Rupert Wilde, he's bound to have questions.'

'Sanjeewa's an old friend and I've relied on his discretion before. It would be useful for him to be in the know to some extent to report on any visitors Wilde has, or anything he might let slip whilst he's at the hotel.'

'What about the staff and residents? Do you think many people are aware there was an incident?'

'Hard to say, but I'll ask Sanjeewa to ensure that his staff are discreet.'

* * *

After they had spoken to Sanjeewa, de Silva and Hebden left the hotel.

'I'll be interested to hear how this goes on,' said Hebden as they stopped beside his car. 'On a lighter note, I hear Jane plans to learn to drive.'

'I suppose Emerald told you.'

'Yes. In case it's of interest, one of my elderly patients has decided to give up driving. The car is a Morris Minor.

I would think it's the perfect thing for a new driver, and as far as I know, it's in good condition. He's driven it very little in the last couple of years. Would you like me to have a word with him?'

De Silva hesitated and Hebden chuckled. 'I think that once the ladies have set their minds to something, one might as well give in.'

'Hmm, I suppose you're right. Let me have a word with Jane first and I'll let you know.'

It was a balmy evening; de Silva drove home slowly so that he could enjoy it. After he left the centre of town and was on the quieter lanes that led to Sunnybank, the Morris's headlights picked out a startled deer that stood frozen by the roadside. He slowed in case it ran in front of the car, but instead it turned and crashed into the bushes. Glad it had escaped, he drove on. Deer often roamed around the area after dark. If they managed to invade any of the gardens, they were particularly fond of munching on roses, but they were such pretty creatures that he tried to forgive them for trespassing.

When he arrived home, he got out of the car and stopped for a few moments to look up at the stars. Away from the more numerous lights of town, the sky was a velvet black; the stars shone like diamonds. He picked out the constellations he knew: Pegasus, the winged horse, the celestial twins, the Gemini, and Cassiopeia, the boastful queen of ancient Greek myth who was punished by Poseidon the sea god for her vanity.

A warm rain began to fall, pattering on the ribbed, paddle-shaped leaves of the banana plants to one side of the bungalow and the pots of scarlet and yellow cannas on either side of the front door. He fished in his pocket for his key and put it in the lock. As he opened the door, Bella emerged from behind the coat stand and came to nudge her nose against his leg.

'I'm sorry you've been kept waiting,' he said, picking her up. She smelled faintly of laundry soap; he tapped her gently on the head. 'Have you been taking a nap on Delisha's clean washing again? I expect that if she caught you, she wasn't pleased.' But he knew that their servant Delisha, who was responsible for the laundry, wouldn't really mind. Like the rest of the household, she was very fond of Bella and her brother Billy.

Jane was on the verandah with Billy dozing beside her chair. He got up and came to greet de Silva then returned to his place and curled up again. The rain was coming down harder now, hissing on the shrubs nearby, gurgling in the gutter and downpipes, and intensifying the scents from the garden.

'Have you eaten?' asked Jane.

'I've not had time. I'm sorry I didn't telephone to say I'd be late. I wasn't expecting to be, but you know how it is.'

'I do. You must be hungry. I'll ask cook to prepare something for you. Will you have a whisky whilst you're waiting?'

'What an excellent idea.' He sank gratefully into his chair and Bella jumped on his lap. Jane went inside and returned a few moments later with his drink. 'The food won't be long. Now, tell me what's been happening.'

'Something that may have thrown a hammer in the works.'

'A spanner, dear.'

'Ah.'

'It's lucky that Rupert Wilde wasn't more seriously hurt,' she said when de Silva had explained about the crash. 'I agree with you, it's strange that he seemed so forgiving. Not at all what one would expect. But if the two of them are in league, it would explain why he doesn't want to bring charges against Eddie.'

'It raises the question of whether Toby Heatherington has anything to do with this business after all.'

Jane pondered for a moment. 'Then why was he at the stables early that morning, and why deny he'd been there before when we met him at the races? I believe Rose when she told us she saw him. I don't think she'd make the story up. If she's fond of Eddie, it must have been very hard for her to say that he might be implicated. Of course, for her sake, one hopes he's not. I wonder what will happen between them. Her parents may not look on him as the kind of man they want their daughter to marry but she'll be twenty-one in a few years and entitled to make her own choices, so they may have to put up with that.'

'I wonder what your parents would have said about me.'

Jane smiled. 'I'm sure they would have grown to love you.'

'Thank you for the vote of confidence, my love.' He took a sip of his whisky.

Their servant Leela appeared in the doorway. 'Will sahib be eating in the dining room?'

'I think I'd rather stay out here.' After the long day, even the effort of moving to the dining room seemed arduous.

'Then please fetch one of the small garden tables and set it up here, Leela,' said Jane.

'Yes, memsahib.'

Soon the table was laid and Leela brought dishes of curry along with a steaming mound of freshly cooked rice. Small bowls contained accompaniments of tomato and mango chutney.

De Silva inhaled the appetising aromas and tucked in. 'Ah that's better,' he said when he had finished his first helpings. 'Dickie and Grace de Jong were keen to take Eddie straight home and I agreed on their assurance that he would be available for me to question him about the crash tomorrow morning. As he was out when I went up to the de Jongs' place in the afternoon, I've not had the chance to find out where he was on the day of the Hill Country

Cup either. As for Toby Heatherington, Dickie de Jong told me he'd left town. Much as I'd still like to question him, it looks like it will have to wait.'

He suddenly remembered the car. 'By the way, David Hebden mentioned that an elderly patient of his has decided to give up driving and has a car to dispose of. David thought it might suit you.'

'Oh, that's exciting. What type of car is it?'

'A Morris Minor. Do you want to see it? If you like it, I think I'll ask Gopallawa to get one of his mechanics to look it over before we make an offer. I need to take the Morris in for one of her tyres to be repaired anyway. I got a puncture on the way up to the de Jongs' plantation and had to change to the spare.'

'You didn't mention that. What a nuisance.'

'It was, but if it hadn't been for that, I would probably have left the plantation before the call came from the Crown, and as Rupert Wilde was so keen not to press charges, I might never have known the accident had taken place.'

'A fortuitous flat you might call it,' said Jane with a smile.

'Yes; now I think I'll have some more of this delicious curry.'

CHAPTER 20

To de Silva's relief, the journey back to the de Jongs' plantation the next morning passed off without incident. As he drove along, he wondered what kind of reception he was about to get. Eddie's parents had been courteous but if their son's mood hadn't changed, it might be hard to persuade him to talk. He remembered the belligerent tone in the young man's voice at Florence and Archie's party at the Residence.

When one of the servants showed him into the drawing room, he was surprised to find that only Grace was waiting for him there. 'Please come in and sit down, Inspector,' she said in her quiet voice. She indicated a chair and sat down on the one opposite. 'I expect you're wondering why my son and my husband aren't joining us. First of all, let me assure you that Eddie hasn't left the house. If you still wish to speak to him when you've heard what I have to say, I'll send one of the servants to fetch him.'

'Thank you, ma'am.'

De Silva waited to hear what she would say next. He noticed that she was very pale and seemed to be struggling to hold herself together. For what seemed like a long time, but was probably only a few moments, she looked down at her hands folded in her lap, then she raised her head. Her eyes met his with such a fierce stare that he couldn't have looked away if he'd wanted to.

'It was because of me that Eddie drove into Rupert's car.'

De Silva's ears pricked up at her use of Wilde's first name. Why would she refer to him by that?

'Have you already guessed my secret, Inspector?' Grace asked dryly. 'Rupert Wilde and I have been having an affair for the past year. I thought we had been discreet, but Eddie found out, and he was furious.' A look of pain came over her face. 'How I wish he'd talked to me. I might have been able to make him see sense. Instead, I found out that he stormed off to confront Rupert. Shortly afterwards, I met Rupert in private at the Clutterbucks' party. He told me that out of concern for my reputation, he'd denied Eddie's allegation, but any hope I had that Eddie would accept Rupert's word was soon dashed. He refused to give up. Yesterday, he tracked Rupert down at his club and insisted on seeing him. He accused Rupert of destroying our family. Apparently, he was drunk. Trying to protect me, Rupert had him removed as discreetly as possible. Eddie left but he waited outside for Rupert to come out. When he did and set off for the Crown where he was due to have dinner with some friends, Eddie followed him. You know the rest.'

For a moment, de Silva wasn't sure how to respond. This was news he hadn't anticipated; nor would he have expected such frankness from a woman who seemed as reserved as Grace de Jong. He wondered how much Dickie knew about her affair.

'Have I shocked you, Inspector? I have to admit, there have been numerous times when I've struggled to excuse my own behaviour.' She flushed. 'But disloyalty in a marriage can work both ways.' She wiped away a tear and he felt pity for her. 'I've put up with my husband's infidelities for longer than I care to remember. His excuse has always been that the ladies involved meant nothing to him, but for me—'

She turned away and a few moments passed before she

faced him again. 'I don't want to burden you with my family's troubles, Inspector. I wouldn't have said anything if it hadn't been necessary to protect Eddie. You will make sure there's no black mark against his name, won't you?' A pleading note came into her voice and again de Silva felt sorry for her. It must have been very hard to make the confession she just had to someone who was virtually a stranger.

'As Mr Wilde doesn't want to press charges, I see no reason why the incident can't be forgotten, ma'am. The manager at the Crown assured me he'll instruct his staff not to talk about it, although I'm afraid some of the guests may already be aware of something untoward.'

Grace shrugged. 'If that's the case, it can't be helped.' She gave him a wan smile. 'I have few friends, Inspector, and none of them close. If necessary, I shall have to endure the gossip of my acquaintances.'

She looked so lonely that it wrung his heart. On the surface, with their wealth, good looks, and elevated position in Nuala society, the de Jongs seemed such a privileged couple. Grace had revealed a different side to their lives.

'I'm sorry to raise it at such a time, ma'am, but I still need to talk to your son about another matter.'

'Oh?'

'I'd like to know what his movements were on the day of the Hill Country Cup.'

'Does this have something to do with the inquiry?' Clearly Grace's distress hadn't blunted her powers of perception. 'Surely that exonerated our family and confirmed that neither of our horses had been tampered with.'

'That was the verdict, ma'am,' de Silva replied carefully, 'but there are other issues involved.'

'I'm not sure I can bear any more bad news at the moment. I hope the result of the inquiry isn't to be set aside.'

'That's not yet decided, ma'am.'

Grace sighed. 'I see. I'll have Eddie brought here. I hope

you have no objection to my remaining whilst you talk to him.'

'Not at all.'

She went over to a bell on the wall and pressed it. When a servant came, she instructed them to fetch Eddie.

* * *

On the drive back to town after his interview with Eddie, who gave a surprisingly lucid account of his activities on the day of the Hill Country Cup, de Silva decided not to go straight on to the station. He needed to clear his head and that would be easier with Jane to talk to.

'Hello, dear, I didn't expect to see you back yet,' she said when he came into the drawing room where she was sitting at her desk writing up her household accounts. She put the cap back on her fountain pen, blotted the page she'd been writing on and closed the ledger. 'The accounts can wait.'

'I hope we can still afford to eat,' de Silva said with a grin.

Jane raised an eyebrow. 'You know perfectly well that I'm very thrifty.'

'I do. I was only joking.'

Jane rolled her eyes. 'So, how did you get on at the de Jongs?'

'Come for a walk around the garden and I'll tell you about it. I'd like some air.'

'Will you wait whilst I change my shoes? The grass is bound to be wet in places after the rain last night.'

'Yes, I expect it will be.'

Billy and Bella, who had been curled up under the desk having a snooze, got up and stretched then came to say hello to de Silva as Jane left the room. When she returned, they followed the two of them into the garden.

Where the sun had shone on it, the grass was dry, but they kept to the shade and there it was still damp. The rain had freshened the trees and shrubs; de Silva inhaled the lush scent of greenery and began to recount what Grace had told him.

'I doubt you were anticipating that,' remarked Jane when he'd finished.

'I certainly wasn't.'

'Will you speak to Rupert Wilde to find out if he corroborates Grace's story?'

De Silva shook his head. 'I suppose I would if I were doing everything according to procedure, but in this case, I believe I can make an exception. I strongly doubt that she would have made such a thing up.'

'That's true. Poor lady, she seems very reserved, and with her position in society it must have been hard to entrust anyone with such personal information, even a policeman. I presume she'll tell Wilde that she's told you about them. I wonder how he'll react.'

'Sympathetically, one hopes,' said de Silva.

'I don't think we can rule out an association between Eddie and his friend Toby yet, but it seems unlikely that Eddie and Wilde conspired to dope Garnet and Bright Star to make money, as Edmund Fallowfield suggested. Once Eddie found out about his mother and Wilde, they wouldn't have been on good terms. Maybe Wilde's reaction to Edmund Fallowfield's remark about Sunil not being someone to trust with one's darkest secrets simply touched a nerve because Wilde had his affair with Grace to hide and thought Fallowfield might have heard rumours and been alluding to it.'

De Silva considered the idea for a few moments. 'Why would Fallowfield want to make trouble for Wilde? He doesn't seem to be the kind of man who indulges in idle gossip. In fact quite the reverse. I have the impression he doesn't much like mixing with other people.'

'Jealousy? Perhaps because he thinks that Wilde's wealthier and more successful socially.'

'But if jealousy is what's behind it and Fallowfield has no hard evidence, he would be taking a considerable risk accusing Wilde. There is such a thing as defamation of character.' De Silva paused for a moment. 'I noticed something when I went to see him at his house. He has some interesting old cars and I stopped to take a better look at them before I left. I happened to see some rags at the back of the garage where they were parked. They were stained, either with dirt or blood, I'm not sure which. I couldn't take a closer look because Fallowfield turned up, but that's something I'd like to do. There was blood on Sunil's body when it was found.'

'I suppose there might be a connection,' said Jane thoughtfully. 'We haven't really considered Fallowfield before. How do you propose to have a better look at these rags?'

'If I go back in the daytime, it's likely someone will be around, and I don't have a plausible excuse. It will have to be after dark.'

Jane looked concerned. 'Be careful, won't you?'

'Always, my love.'

They returned to the bungalow, passing the gnarled apple tree through which clambered a white rambling rose. De Silva stopped to tuck in a stray branch. Duty must come first, but he'd be glad to have more time to spend in the garden. The thought reminded him that he'd done nothing about the car David Hebden had told him of.

'Why don't I speak to David myself,' said Jane when he mentioned it.

'That's a good idea. If his patient agrees, Jayasena can collect it and take it in to Gopallawa. I'd like to have it checked before you start to drive it, especially if it hasn't been used for some time.'

'I'll telephone David. Jayasena has already thought of

some quiet roads that would be perfect places for me to begin my lessons.' She grinned and clapped her hands. 'Oh, Shanti. This is so exciting. I'm so looking forward to being able to drive.'

De Silva couldn't help smiling back. How fortunate he was, he thought, unlike so many others.

CHAPTER 21

'It's lucky there's a new moon tonight,' said de Silva as he and Jane ate dinner. 'It should make it easier to keep out of sight.'

'Fallowfield's sure to have at least one night watchman though.'

'Let's hope he's not too vigilant. Fortunately, I didn't see any dogs about the place when I went up there.'

At ten o'clock, he dressed in dark trousers and a dark jacket that buttoned up to the neck and drove to Fallowfield's bungalow. On his previous visit he had noticed a place just before the entrance where one could park, so he left the Morris there and continued on foot, keeping to the trees as much as possible. Once, a loud rustling in the undergrowth made his heartbeat speed up but it was only a monitor lizard disturbed by his passing. Careful as he was not to make a noise, the creature had probably sensed the vibration of his footfall. He was glad the night was cloudy for that dimmed the brilliance of the stars.

When the bungalow came into sight, he stopped and surveyed the scene. Everything was very quiet and there was only one light in an upstairs window. Fallowfield might still be awake but hopefully he wouldn't take it into his head to look out.

The gate across the drive had been open when he last came but now it was closed. There were bolts at the top and bottom, but he didn't want to get in that way. He noticed that the gate had dropped on its hinges and might not open quietly. Instead, he found a spot where a fence post had come out of the ground and lay on its side, stretching out the wire fencing that was nailed to it so that it was almost flat on the ground. De Silva blessed the animal that had, no doubt, caused the damage and proceeded to step carefully across the wire.

Unfortunately, his route was soon impeded by an enormous yucca. He tried to give it a wide berth but misjudged the distance in the gloom and one of the sharp spiny leaves sliced his hand. He winced and snatched it away then put it to his mouth. There was the metallic taste of blood. With his other hand, he pulled his handkerchief from his pocket to use as a bandage.

A few more steps and the open-fronted garage where he had seen the rags was in sight. Both cars were still parked there. He went to the spot where the distance between the tree cover and the entrance was the narrowest, took a deep breath and stole across. It was even darker inside the garage than it had been outside. He waited until his eyes became accustomed to the lower level of light. He was feeling his way along the side of the first car when a low, haunting sound made his blood freeze. There was a swish of air, and a shadow passed over him. *Probably just an owl*, he told himself. Sure enough, when he looked in the direction where the shadow had gone, he saw a squat shape with a pair of yellow saucer eyes perched on a beam. This time, his heartbeat took longer to slow down. He was getting too old for this kind of escapade.

He walked past the second car to the corner where he had seen the suspicious rags. There was nothing there except dust and cobwebs, one of which wrapped itself around his head in a sticky embrace. He fought it off and dusted his hands on his trousers before checking the rest of the garage, but all he encountered was a small pile of logs presumably destined for a fire, a petrol can, and a row of hooks from which hung a hammer, a small axe, and a saw. Had he imagined the stained rags? No, he was sure they had been there.

A cough came from the entrance to the garage, making his blood freeze once more. He crouched down between the cars and waited, trying to ignore the pain in his knees. Whoever was out there started to whistle tunelessly, then there was a brief flare of light followed by silence. Perhaps they were lighting a cigarette, or rather, from the smell that soon reached his nostrils, a beedi, one of the thin cigarettes made of tobacco, herbs and betel nut that were popular with people who needed a cheap smoke.

The smoker, presumably a night watchman, seemed in no hurry to move on. De Silva groaned inwardly. How much longer was he going to have to stay squashed up like a frog under a stone? Another bout of coughing ensued and the sound of a gobbet of phlegm being hawked up. Someone should tell this fellow that smoking was probably killing him, thought de Silva irritably.

Five minutes later, minutes that each seemed like a year to de Silva, the smell of beedi began to fade. The night watchman must have finished his smoke. The tuneless whistling recommenced but it grew fainter by the moment. With luck the man was moving on. De Silva waited until there was silence then rose stiffly to his feet, rubbing his calves to bring the blood back into them.

On the way back to the Morris, he puzzled over the significance of the missing rags. Did they provide a clue? As there had been blood on Sunil's body when it was found, might they have been used to wipe away some that had got on the murderer's hands?

Then another thought occurred to him. He remembered how, when they'd met on the day that Sunil's body had been found, Fallowfield had kept one hand in his pocket all the time. Yet at their later meeting, he had lit a cigarette using both hands, and it was clear from the nicotine stains on his fingers that he was a heavy smoker. Why had he abstained the previous time? The meeting in his office at the racecourse had lasted for a considerable length of time. He recalled that Fallowfield had offered him tea and they'd sat and talked about his background. Was it pure chance that he never lit a cigarette, or could it be that he was hiding an injury? Perhaps one he had sustained when damaging the ladder that Sunil fell from? He might have cut himself with an axe if that was what he used, but on reflection that was unlikely because an axe would have caused a serious injury that would have been obvious to all. There would also have been blood on the remains of the rung.

A more likely possibility was that he'd caught his hand on something – a hook or a nail perhaps – as he was moving the ladder and letting it drop onto Sunil's body, giving the weakened rung a final kick to create the splintered break, if, indeed, that's what happened. Shanti remembered the bridles hanging on hooks and nails in the darkened barn and thought how difficult and hazardous it would be to get the ladder into the right position if one was trying to manoeuvre such a heavy object on one's own in poor light. Had Fallowfield used the rags to staunch the blood on his hand, just as de Silva had wrapped his handkerchief around his own hand when the yucca cut it? If so, the rags had lain forgotten in the corner of the garage, until seeing de Silva there reminded Fallowfield, and he decided to dispose of them in case anyone asked awkward questions about whose blood it was and how it came to be spilt.

The visit had provided plenty to think about and to discuss with Jane, but it was well past midnight when he reached home, and they were both tired. They agreed to discuss the missing rags in the morning.

CHAPTER 22

Over an early breakfast of soft-boiled eggs, tea, and toast, de Silva told Jane about the visit to Fallowfield's house in more detail. 'So, I'm not sure where to go from here,' he finished. 'I fear we may not have paid enough attention to Fallowfield, but better late than never. I'd like to find out more about him.'

'If he's our man, what would be his motive?'

'Money is the obvious one, and in the case of Sunil's death, like the others, the need to hide his tracks, but at present we've no evidence that he's short of money, despite his modest accommodation.'

'I suppose he would have the opportunity. He knows the stables well and his presence there wouldn't be suspicious.'

'And as for the means, he claims to have been involved in the racing business for many years.' De Silva thought for a moment. 'He also told me that at one time he'd been in the military police in Burma. He described the job as a messy business. I imagine by that he meant he had to carry out some unpleasant tasks. If so, he might have no qualms about murder.'

Jane shuddered. 'Poor Sunil. I hope he didn't suffer.'

'But all this is mere conjecture,' de Silva said gloomily, stirring sugar into his second cup of tea.

'There must be some way of finding out about his background.'

'Hmm.' There was a pause then he brightened. 'I have an idea: Archie's brother.'

'What about him?'

'Archie mentioned that he's extremely keen on racing. I wonder if he'd have contacts who might know something about Fallowfield's past life. It's a long shot, but I can't think of a better idea.'

'I'm not sure if he and his wife are still in Nuala, but if not, I'm sure Archie would speak to him on the telephone.'

'It's about time I brought Archie up to date anyway. I'll make a call to the Residence and find out if he's free to see me today.'

'Good idea. Oh, by the way, I spoke with David Hebden about the car as we agreed. He was very helpful and promised to talk to his patient as soon as possible. He promised that if he didn't manage to ring back yesterday to let me know how he was getting on, he would do so this morning.'

'Excellent. At least it sounds as if something is going smoothly.'

Jane reached across the table and laid a hand on his. 'You mustn't be discouraged. I'm sure the case will soon be solved.'

'I hope so.' He drained the last of his tea and stood up. 'An excellent breakfast as always. Now, I'd better make that call.'

* * *

Rose Appleby was also up early that morning. She wanted to take Slipper out for some exercise before she went to work. She was determined not to neglect the mare, even though as she parked her car in the yard, the thought that Sunil wouldn't be waiting to greet her, his big smile splitting his face from ear to ear, brought tears to her eyes.

She had so many conflicting feelings about Eddie, too. He hadn't been in touch with her for over a week. Part of her longed to see him, but the other part was glad not to have to face him. She was still unsure about whether he'd had a hand in Sunil's death.

'Good morning!'

Her heart sank as she recognised Edmund Fallowfield's voice. She was convinced now that he didn't really want to find out what had happened to Sunil, and she had no desire to talk to him. She must think of a way to get rid of him as quickly as possible. She forced a smile. 'Good morning, Mr Fallowfield.'

'Edmund, please.' He came over and held the car door open for her, standing so close as she got out that she smelled his cologne. She stepped away quickly and he gave her an awkward smile.

'I've been hoping to hear from you, Rose.'

'Oh?'

'Our conversation the other day – I asked if you would share any information you uncovered about Sunil's death.'

Rose took a deep breath. 'I'm sorry if I gave you the wrong impression. I was very upset after it happened, but now I've had more time to come to terms with Sunil's death, I've decided I was probably wrong about it not being an accident. I think it's best to put the whole thing behind me. Now, if you'll excuse me, I came up to exercise Slipper and I don't have a great deal of time.'

* * *

Archie was busy when de Silva telephoned the Residence, but his secretary promised to speak to him. She rang back not long afterwards to tell him that Archie would be free in an hour.

When he arrived at the Residence, one of the servants directed de Silva to the fishing lake. 'The sahib and his brother are down there now,' he said. 'Shall I take you to them?'

'Thank you, I can find my own way.'

The lake shimmered like a silver plate in the sunshine. Swelled by the recent heavy rain, the water had risen further than usual up the little beach at the bottom of the track. There was no sign of Archie and his brother so he decided to walk in a clockwise direction towards the side of the lake where the bank had more shade, hoping that was where they would be. The narrow path wound its way between trees and undergrowth. On the lakeside, some of the trees had grown almost horizontally, snaking out across water dappled with gold-green light.

After a minute or two, de Silva heard the hissing sound of a fishing line being cast out then a buzz as it was reeled in. A few more yards and Archie and his brother came into sight. They were admiring an iridescent blue fish with orange markings that Archie had just caught. He reached out with a net on a long pole and brought it to land. Although de Silva often ate fish, he couldn't help but wince as Archie brought out his gamekeeper's priest and briskly whacked the fish on the head before dropping it into the wicker creel at his side.

A stick cracked under de Silva's foot and both men looked around.

'Ah, de Silva! We've been expecting you. Come and meet my brother, Wilfred. Wilfred, this is Inspector de Silva, our local chief of police.'

Wilfred laid down his rod and stood up. He was a shorter, more dapper version of Archie. De Silva stepped forward to shake his outstretched hand.

'A pleasure to meet you, Inspector.'

'Likewise, sir.'

'Luckily for you, Wilfred and I decided not to go further afield for our fishing today,' said Archie.

'Although we've enjoyed some memorable expeditions,' remarked his brother. 'Unfortunately, however, my wife and I have to leave Nuala tomorrow.'

Archie got to his feet. 'You're in time for a drink and a bite to eat, de Silva.' He beckoned to some of the Residence's servants who were sitting on a fallen tree trunk a little way off, and cupped a hand around his mouth. 'You can bring lunch out now,' he called.

Cold beers and sandwiches were produced and placed on a camping table around which the servants arranged three folding chairs. De Silva accepted a beer, and not wishing to be impolite, also took a sandwich. The filling was pink and slightly rubbery. He guessed it was luncheon meat.

'Well, fire away,' said Archie after the servants had withdrawn to their fallen tree trunk and one of them had gone off to the house with the morning's catch. He took a bite of his sandwich – from the fishy smell that reached de Silva's sensitive nostrils, he presumed that filling was tinned sardine.

The brothers listened as de Silva outlined his thoughts about Edmund Fallowfield. He wasn't sure Wilfred was entirely convinced that there was good reason to be suspicious.

'I see,' said Archie slowly when de Silva had finished. 'Finding out about this fellow sounds more up your street than mine, Wilfred.' He looked at his brother. 'It may seem a bit far-fetched, but I've good reason to trust de Silva's instincts. What do you say?'

'I'll see what I can do.'

'By the way, de Silva, I've had no luck finding out more about that fellow Heatherington. Anything from your end?'

'No, sir.'

Archie shrugged. 'If you're on the right lines with

Fallowfield, Heatherington may not be important anyway. Anything else to report?'

De Silva wished he didn't have to reveal Grace's secret, but it was relevant to the case and that left him no choice.

Archie looked grave. 'Embarrassing for the whole family as well as Wilde,' he said when de Silva had finished. 'We'd better keep this to ourselves, don't you think? Still, useful information. It may be that Fallowfield was deliberately trying to lead us up the wrong path. Let's see what can be done to find out if he was and why.'

CHAPTER 23

After he left the Residence, de Silva decided to go home for lunch. The sandwich hadn't been very sustaining, and it would give him the opportunity to tell Jane what had happened, but when he arrived at Sunnybank, she was out.

'The memsahib has gone to a meeting of one of her committees, sahib,' said Delisha. 'She said she wouldn't be back until teatime.'

Briefly, de Silva wondered whether to go to the bazaar and buy himself something to fill the gap left by the sandwich, but he didn't feel like eating amidst all the noise and bustle.

'Never mind, I'll just have to have lunch on my own. Please tell cook I'm here.'

'Yes, sahib.' She left the room and returned a few moments later. 'Cook says he can make curried fish and rice quickly, sahib.'

'That will do very well.'

Whilst he waited for his meal, de Silva thought about the morning's work. Amongst other things, he wondered how much Dickie de Jong knew about his wife's affair and how he had taken it. Eddie's remark at the Clutterbucks' party about his father having no right to judge others came back to him; did it mean that Eddie knew that Dickie had also been unfaithful?

He was halfway through his meal when Delisha came in to tell him that David Hebden was on the telephone.

'Sorry to drag you away from your lunch, de Silva,' he said jovially. 'I was just calling to let you and Jane know that my patient's Morris Minor is at Gopallawa Motors.'

'Excellent, thank you for arranging it. I'll look in there this afternoon. It'll be a good opportunity to have one of my tyres mended too. I had a puncture the other day, so I haven't a spare.'

'Not to be recommended on hill country roads.'

'Precisely. Jane seems very keen on this car. Has your patient named a figure with which he'd be satisfied?'

Hebden gave him one that didn't sound too alarming. 'But I suggest you wait and make an offer when the garage has had a look,' he added.

'I will.'

* * *

As usual, it was sweltering and noisy at Gopallawa's garage; the air smelled of petrol and axle grease. Gopallawa himself came out from the untidy back office to greet de Silva.

'Good afternoon, Inspector. I've put one of my men onto looking over this car for you. It shouldn't take long.'

'Thank you. I have another job that needs doing as well.' He explained about the puncture.

'He can see to that when he's finished with the other car. We close at six. If you'd like to leave the Morris with us, both jobs should be done by then.'

'Excellent.'

De Silva went out to the street and hailed a passing rickshaw to take him to the police station. He spent a while talking with Prasanna and Nadar and looking over paperwork, but his mind kept straying back to Edmund Fallowfield. He didn't blame Archie's brother for being somewhat sceptical about the idea that he might be the murderer, but it gave him considerable satisfaction to know that Archie himself hadn't dismissed his theory. 'Though goodness knows what to do next if Wilfred comes up with nothing,' he muttered.

Just after five, he let Prasanna and Nadar go home, locked the station, and set off for Gopallawa's garage.

'Your car is ready,' said Gopallawa when he arrived. 'My mechanic has also finished looking at the other one. All in order and I'd say the price is fair. Shall we walk over, and I can show it to you?'

In the workshop at the back of the garage, they passed a badly damaged car. De Silva wondered if it might be the one that Rupert Wilde had been driving when Eddie ran into him outside the Crown hotel.

'A bad mess,' remarked Gopallawa. 'It will take a lot of work to fix it.' He indicated the twisted back bumper and crumpled open boot. 'This must all be hammered out and the lock replaced.'

'Does it belong to a sahib called Wilde?'

'Yes; you know about the accident?'

'I was there.'

Gopallawa shrugged. 'Young men are careless.'

He moved on and de Silva was about to follow when he noticed that although the inside of the boot was spotless, no doubt the work of Wilde's servants, there was a small bundle of dirty rags there. It occurred to him that he'd seen them before but no, surely it was just a coincidence. Perhaps one of the mechanics had left them behind.

Gopallawa looked back over his shoulder. 'Is something wrong, sahib?'

De Silva shook his head. 'Lead on.'

The Morris Minor that was being offered for sale had pale green paintwork with a cream roof.

'There are a few paint chips,' said Gopallawa, pointing one out, 'but they can be touched up.'

De Silva opened the passenger door and looked inside. The walnut dashboard looked freshly polished and the tan leather seats were in reasonable condition for the car's age. Gopallawa lifted the bonnet and propped it open. 'The engine is in good order. I think your wife should have no troubles.'

'I'm glad to hear it. Thank you for doing this. You must tell me what I owe.'

'On the house, sahib. You need only pay for the mended tyre.'

'Thank you. I'll come back to your office and do that now.'

On the way past Wilde's car, however, he paused and looked again at the rags.

'Is something wrong, sahib?'

De Silva reached into the boot and picked them up. 'Were these in here when the car was brought in?'

'I'm not sure. Balan worked on the car. I'll ask him.' Gopallawa called out in Tamil to one of the mechanics who replied that he thought they had been.

'I'd like to take them with me.'

Gopallawa looked puzzled but he nodded.

'Good. Keep this between the two of us, please.'

'Very well, sahib.'

As de Silva followed him to the office to pay his bill, he studied the rags thoughtfully. What interested him was that along with the dirt, they had several other stains on them. He was pretty sure they were the same ones that he'd seen in Edmund Fallowfield's garage.

* * *

'Telephone call for you, Rose,' Jed Fraser called out as she was putting on her hat and getting ready to leave the office.

She'd agreed to have dinner with Eddie, who had finally called, and had spent a considerable portion of the afternoon trying to decide how she felt about him. He'd said he had something important he wanted to discuss.

'Who is it?'

Jed held out the receiver. 'Says his name's Masham.'

Rose was puzzled. Why would Pat Masham be calling her? She hoped nothing was the matter with Slipper. She took the receiver from Jed. 'Hello, Pat. Is anything wrong?'

Masham's lilting Irish brogue came down the line. 'Can you get up here?'

Rose felt a chill come over her. 'Is it Slipper?'

'No, no, it's not that. I need to show you something. It's about the poor lad Sunil.'

'What?'

'I can't talk on the telephone. Meet me in the barn where he was found. Best not to tell anyone you're coming.'

Rose hesitated. It was a strange request, especially coming from Pat, but he might have found out something important. 'Alright.'

She put down the phone and saw that Jed was grinning. 'In demand tonight, eh?'

'What do you mean?'

'Thought you were meeting your boyfriend.'

'Who told you that?'

'Just a guess.'

'As it happens, I am.'

'I can give him a message if you like. That's if he's coming to pick you up here. I won't be leaving for a bit.'

Rose forced a smile. Annoying as he often was, for once Jed did seem to be trying to be helpful. 'Thank you. I have to go somewhere for a little while. Will you tell him I'll meet him at the Crown instead? Say I shouldn't be very late.'

CHAPTER 24

As de Silva drove home, his head was full of the hypothesis that his find at the garage had inspired. He hoped Jane would be back; he was eager to try it out on her. The first part of it assumed that Fallowfield had broken Sunil's neck to make it seem as if he'd died in a fall from the ladder. He had damaged the ladder before or after the event and cut his hand when he was moving it to let it drop onto Sunil's body, using the rags that were now in Rupert Wilde's car to stop the bleeding. When he saw de Silva in the garage at his bungalow, it had reminded him that he hadn't disposed of the rags. He might not have realised, however, that de Silva had noticed them.

From early on, and for reasons de Silva couldn't yet fathom, Fallowfield had been keen to put the blame for Sunil's death on Wilde. Had he found an opportunity to put the rags in Wilde's car, his plan being that he would find a way of drawing attention to them, perhaps by repeating his allegation against Wilde and suggesting de Silva search his property, including his car? Bloodied rags in his car could be construed as evidence that Wilde had somehow got blood from Sunil's injured face on his hands and needed to wipe it away. At the very least it would promote a more in-depth investigation into Wilde's involvement and throw more suspicion onto him.

Since Wilde was vague about where he was on the evening

of the party at the Residence, I might have been persuaded to instigate a search, thought de Silva. *Except now I know that the reason why Wilde didn't want to tell me exactly what he'd been doing was because he spent some of the time having a private talk with Grace de Jong.*

At Sunnybank, he let himself in and saw Jane's hat on the stand in the hall. There were lights in the drawing room. She must be home. A moment later she came out to greet him. There was an anxious expression on her face.

'Oh good, Shanti, you're back.'

'You look worried. Is something wrong?'

'I'm not sure. It may be nothing, but George Appleby telephoned. He said he'd tried to call the police station but there was no answer.'

'What was so urgent?' asked de Silva, feeling puzzled.

'Rose is missing. She was supposed to be having dinner with Eddie de Jong, but when he went to fetch her, there no one at the newspaper office apart from the caretaker, who said that she'd already left. She hasn't come home either. The Applebys were afraid she might have had an accident. That was why George telephoned the station. He wanted to find out if there'd been a report of one.'

'Not that I know of.'

'I suppose Rose might have changed her mind about spending the evening with Eddie but if she did and didn't go home either, where *did* she go?'

A nasty suspicion came into de Silva's mind. 'I hope I'm wrong, but she might be in danger.'

'Why do you say that?'

'I warned her not to ask any more questions about the Hill Country Cup inquiry and Sunil's death, but if she ignored my advice, she may have put herself at risk.' He explained about the rags in Wilde's car and his theory about Edmund Fallowfield. 'If I'm right and he's worked out that Rose is onto him, it may be Fallowfield who's with her now.

I think we'd better head for the newspaper office and see if we can get any more information from the caretaker. I'll explain on the way.'

* * *

When they reached the office of the *Nuala Times*, there was no sign of the caretaker. 'I'll try around the back,' said de Silva.

Jane put a hand on his sleeve. 'Look, there's someone coming. He doesn't look like a caretaker, but he might know something.'

'Good evening to you,' the man nodded to them.

'Do you work here?'

'Yes, Jed Fraser's the name. Are you looking for someone?'

'Your caretaker. We're trying to find out where Rose Appleby's got to.'

'Rose?' A slightly defensive tone came into Jed's voice. 'She asked me to give a message to her boyfriend to say she'd be late. I haven't missed him, have I? I've only been gone a couple of minutes. Needed a packet of ciggies.'

De Silva suspected Fraser had been gone for a lot more than a few minutes, but he didn't comment. The important thing was to find Rose. 'Did she tell you where she was going?'

'No, but someone telephoned her just before she left. Said his name was Masham.'

'Pat Masham?'

Jed shrugged. 'Might have been.'

De Silva reached into his pocket for his notebook, tore a page out and scribbled a telephone number on it. He handed it to Jed. 'Please call this number. It's Rose's home. Ask for her father, George. Tell him Inspector de Silva and his wife are going up to the stables at the racecourse. We think Rose may be there and needing help.'

Jed took the paper and glanced at it. 'Alright, I'll tell him.' He looked up. 'Hey! Wait for me! What's the story?' But de Silva and Jane didn't answer. They were already on their way to the Morris.

'If she's gone to the racecourse,' said Jane, 'It won't be for a ride. It's far too dark. Do you think there's something the matter with her horse?'

They got into the Morris and de Silva switched on the engine. 'It seems unlikely. If the horse was sick, why didn't she call her father and ask him to come with her?'

'As George is a vet, that does seem logical.'

'I'm not convinced the man calling her was Pat Masham.'

'Are you suggesting it was Fallowfield impersonating him?' asked Jane.

'I think there's a strong possibility.' He put his foot down hard on the accelerator. 'If I'm right, let's hope we're in time to rescue her. As a precaution, I think we'd better go to the station first. I may need my gun.'

* * *

Rose's heartbeat quickened as she made the journey up to the racecourse. Soon she might have the answer to her questions about Eddie. Her grip on the steering wheel tightened and her palms were damp with sweat. When she reached the stables, there were no other cars in the yard but that didn't surprise her. It was only a short walk from there to the cottage where Pat Masham lived. The door of the hay barn was closed but a dim light filtered out from around its edges. She lifted the heavy metal ring that worked the latch. The door creaked as it opened.

'Pat? It's me. Rose.'

No answer. She stepped inside, closed the door behind her and peered into the gloom. A single hurricane lamp hung from one of the beams, its light barely disturbing the shadows. There was the usual musty smell of hay and dust.

'Pat? Where—' Her next words were smothered as something rough and scratchy was clamped over her face; it had a foul chemical smell. A strong arm snaked around her waist, preventing her from escaping. Struggling to breathe, she tried to free herself, but her assailant's grip tightened. Pinpricks of light danced in front of her eyes. Her head reeled as darkness descended and her body went limp.

* * *

When she slowly returned to consciousness, she found herself face down on a pile of hay. Its sharp blades scratched her, and something pressed on her back, preventing her from getting up. She tried to push it away only to realise that her hands were tied.

'I wouldn't bother to struggle,' said a voice.

'You're not Pat!'

'How perceptive of you.'

She gave a little gasp as with a desperate effort, she raised her head and pain shot through her neck. Edmund Fallowfield stood a few paces away with a silk scarf bunched in his hands.

'I hope you'll forgive the discourteous welcome, my dear Rose.'

'You! Where's Pat?'

'All in good time.' He bent down and tied the scarf over her mouth. 'Just in case you were thinking of shouting for help. Not that there would be much point. There's no one else up here and Pat won't be joining us. He wasn't the one who telephoned you, I was. I flatter myself I managed a rather good imitation of his accent.'

He smiled. 'Are you really surprised to see me? You've

worked things out, haven't you? One minute you were telling Masham that Sunil might have been murdered, you see I overheard more of your conversation with him than I admitted to, but then you changed your tune with me. Did you think I'd believe that story about your being too upset by your little halfwit friend's death to think straight? As for Masham, all his denying responsibility so as not to have a black mark against his name over that ladder will be useful when I lay the blame on him, and dead men make convenient scapegoats.' He paused. 'Of course, I wouldn't have needed to get rid of the halfwit as well if he hadn't been snooping around. I used a trick I learned in my days in Burma to break his neck then I made it look like an accident.'

A chill came over Rose. So Fallowfield had murdered Sunil and Pat too.

'As for the rest of your precious racing friends. It wasn't hard to fool them. What a joke! Their feeble inquiry was never going to catch me out. It was disappointing though that the worthy Inspector de Silva didn't take the bait over Rupert Wilde.' His lip curled. 'Wilde's a type I particularly despise. Arrogant men who've done nothing to deserve their privileges. Some of us have had to work for every penny we've got, and people like him still treat us as if we were servants. But you—' He bent down and brushed his fingers lightly over her neck. 'I thought you might be different from the rest of your class. It's a pity I was wrong. It saddens me that I have to kill you, but you've left me no choice.'

Rose struggled to speak through the scarf, and he stroked her hair. 'Hush, you needn't be afraid. I'll make it quick as I did for Sunil. I'm not a brute. You won't feel any pain.'

The barn door creaked.

'Step away from her, Fallowfield, and put your hands above your head,' de Silva said loudly.

Fallowfield jumped up and swung around. De Silva stood in the doorway, the gun in his hand pointed at Fallowfield's chest. 'I'll shoot if I have to. Step away from her!'

For a moment Fallowfield hesitated then he launched himself towards the small door at the back of the barn. De Silva fired into the gloom, but the bullet missed, pinging off one of the wooden posts that supported the hayloft. He gave chase, just catching up with Fallowfield as he tried to slam the door in de Silva's face.

They struggled for a few moments then de Silva managed to trip Fallowfield and wrestle him to the ground where he landed face-first with a yell. De Silva yanked his wrists behind his back and handcuffed him. 'Edmund Fallowfield,' he gasped, 'you're under arrest.'

Jane ran into the barn. Still panting from his exertions, de Silva shot her a glance. 'You promised me you'd stay in the car.'

'I heard a gunshot. I had to know if you were safe.' She hurried over to Rose and untied her. 'Oh, you poor girl. You must have been terrified. Are you alright?'

'I … I think so.' Rose began to cry then angrily dashed the tears from her eyes. 'He killed Sunil and I think he's killed Pat as well.'

'Let's get you somewhere more comfortable,' said Jane soothingly, putting an arm under Rose's elbow to help her up. 'Once we've done that you can tell us everything.'

There were footsteps outside the barn and George Appleby rushed in followed by Eddie and Jed Fraser.

'Good God!' George exploded. 'What the hell is going on here?' He hurried over to Rose who was by now on her feet and put his arms around her. She buried her face in his shoulder. 'I'm alright, Pa,' she said in a muffled voice. 'Inspector de Silva and Jane saved me.'

CHAPTER 25

Late the following evening.
Sunnybank

'Rose was admirably calm today, despite her ordeal,' said de Silva. He sat on the edge of his and Jane's bed, the sock he had just taken off bunched in one hand. 'I took her statement this afternoon. She told me about the conversations she had with Fallowfield. I think that at first, he believed she only had a general suspicion that Garnet and Bright Star had been doped and poor Sunil murdered, so at that stage he hoped to steer the investigation towards Wilde or the de Jongs. When she started to rebuff him, however, he came around to the view that she thought he was the culprit. No doubt he was attracted to her, as most men would be, but she misunderstood what he wanted and how he was reading her behaviour. He decided to silence her and chose Masham as his scapegoat.' He yawned and rubbed his eyes with the other hand.

'And her mistake was one that almost cost Rose her life,' said Jane. 'You've had a long day,' she added sympathetically. 'Are you too tired to talk more about it?'

'No, although I warn you, I may fall asleep the second my head touches the pillow.' He paused for a moment. 'Where was I? Ah, yes, Rose was right that Toby Heatherington wasn't what he seemed. It turns out the Jockey Club in

Colombo sent him to investigate Fallowfield, who worked there before he came to Nuala. Some time ago, the Colombo club's officials became suspicious that someone was doping horses. Unlike here in Nuala, a couple of tests came back positive, but no culprit was identified.'

He pulled off the other sock, stood up and dropped both of them onto the bedroom chair where he had already discarded the rest of his clothes. 'Back in a minute.'

Clad in his pyjamas and slippers, he padded down the passage to the bathroom and returned a few moments later halfway through brushing his teeth. 'When Fallowfield left Colombo, the incidents didn't recur. That gave the officials the idea he might be their man. Toby was chosen to investigate. It helped that he's genuinely old friends with Eddie de Jong, but Eddie had no idea of the real reason why he'd come to Nuala.' He finished brushing his teeth and went back to the bathroom to rinse his mouth.

'How do you know all this?' called Jane.

De Silva reappeared. 'Because Archie's brother Wilfred has proved invaluable.' He climbed into bed, settling the pillows comfortably behind his head. 'He's already come up with plenty of useful information.'

'How clever of him. Go on.'

'On the morning Rose saw Toby, he was trying to shadow Fallowfield. He guessed he'd be up to no good on the day of such an important race. He waited near Fallowfield's bungalow for him to drive up to the racecourse, but presumably Fallowfield suspected he was being watched. He gave Toby the slip and must just have had time to get to the stables and administer the drugs to the de Jongs' horses then go to his office before Toby caught up with him.'

'Has he tampered with any other horses here in Nuala?'

'Not that he's admitting to, but according to Wilfred's informants, before Fallowfield lived in Colombo, he was in India. The informants believe he was part of an organised crime syndicate there, but he fell out with them. Perhaps he hoped he would be forgotten if he moved to Ceylon.'

'Do you think he'll agree to talk about this syndicate?'

De Silva shrugged. 'It's worth a try although so far, he's not been very talkative to say the least. Still, soon he won't be our problem anyway. The plan is to transfer him to Colombo and hand him over for further questioning by the police down there.'

He undid the leather strap of his watch and put it down on the bedside table next to his alarm clock and the book he was reading. 'I think the main obstacle that stands in the way of getting him to talk is likely to be the fact that the court can hardly treat leniently someone who murdered two people and threatened to murder a third, so he may continue to stay silent out of sheer spite.'

Pat Masham had been found dead at his cottage with a gun in his hand.

'I see that will make things difficult. Of course, Rose's testimony will be enough to convict him of the two murders and the attempted murder, won't it?'

'Indeed.'

De Silva leaned over to kiss her cheek then moved down the bed and pulled the sheet up to his chin. He thought what a relief it was that the long day was over.

'What about Pat Masham?' asked Jane. 'Has Fallowfield said anything more about why he killed him?'

'As I said, it was hard to get Fallowfield to talk, but according to Rose, he said Masham was a convenient person for him to use as a scapegoat for his crimes. Presumably, he'd given up the idea of incriminating Wilde. Prasanna and Nadar found a letter in Masham's bungalow. It was ostensibly written by him, but I'm convinced that Fallowfield wrote it himself. It had Masham confessing that he'd drugged Bright Star and Garnet. He also claimed he'd murdered Sunil and Rose because he believed they were going to expose him but then he was overcome with remorse and decided to end his own life. No doubt once Fallowfield had killed Rose, he was going to put the letter with Masham's body.'

'Do you think he was just after money?'

'I imagine he would have liked to have more than he could legitimately earn, but I suspect that wasn't the most important thing to him. I believe that what he wanted even more was revenge on the people he thought looked down on him. My guess is that he thought people like Wilde and Dickie de Jong lived in a cocoon of smug comfort, whereas the odds were always against him. He wanted to smash that cocoon and see their reputations in the dust. If there was doubt over the result of the Jockey Club inquiry, and he could influence Archie and me to take him seriously, he might achieve his aim. The murders became necessary when his plan looked to be coming up against obstacles and he was in danger.'

'I wonder if he'd hoped for a fresh start when he came here and had been disillusioned. That would increase his resentment.'

'You're probably right.'

Jane shuddered. 'Just think, if that man Jed Fraser hadn't gone off to buy cigarettes when Eddie came to call for Rose, he would probably have given Eddie the message and Eddie would have gone away to wait at the Crown. A lot more time might have passed before anyone raised the alarm and Fallowfield would have had the chance to carry out his plan.'

'Fate moves in a mysterious way.' He reached for the bedside light switch and turned the light out. 'Goodnight, my love. Let's talk more in the morning.'

'Sleep well, dear.'

CHAPTER 26

A few days later

'I hope you don't mind my coming unannounced like this, Mrs de Silva,' said Rose.

'Of course not, my dear, I'm delighted to see you. And there's no need to stand on ceremony. Do call me Jane.'

'Thank you.'

'You look well. I hope you're recovering from your ordeal. What a horrible experience for you.'

'It was, but I'm starting to feel a little better. Everyone has been so kind, but more than anything, I want to thank you and your husband again. Without you—'

Jane squeezed her hand. 'Try not to think about that. You're safe now. Will you stay awhile? We can sit on the verandah, and I'll have some tea brought out. Shanti will be back soon. I know he'd be very sorry to miss you.'

'And I him,' said Rose. 'Thank you, tea would be lovely.'

'Excellent.'

'I expect your husband's told you that Edmund Fallowfield has been taken to the jail in Colombo,' said Rose when the tea had been brought. The garden drooped in the heat of the afternoon sun but in the shade of the verandah, it was pleasantly cool.

'Yes, he has.'

Rose shuddered. 'I'm very glad that he's gone.'

'I'm sure you are. What a dreadful man.'

'I didn't make a very good job of being a detective, did I? I was too quick to be convinced that Toby Heatherington was involved. If it hadn't been for your husband, my mistake might have been fatal.'

'You shouldn't reproach yourself,' said Jane, deciding it was best not to tell Rose that Toby had been involved but not in the way she thought. 'Shanti has had many years of practice.'

'I suppose he has.' Rose hesitated for a moment. 'I expect you know that Eddie's mother and Rupert Wilde had an affair. It was because of her that your husband decided he was probably on the wrong track when he suspected Eddie.'

'Yes, we did talk about that. In the strictest confidence, naturally.'

'Of course. Poor Eddie. He's very upset about the whole business. He has his father to deal with too. Dickie was furious about Grace's affair, although I'm not convinced it came as a surprise to him. I think he had an idea there was something going on and didn't want to face it.'

Rose raised an eyebrow. 'Between ourselves, Eddie tells me that Dickie hasn't always been faithful himself. Grace has ended her affair with Rupert, and Eddie's determined to persuade Dickie to forgive and forget, as his mother has done on more than one occasion.'

'I'm sure it helps Eddie to have you to confide in.'

Rose flushed.

'I'm so sorry,' Jane said quickly. 'I didn't mean to pry.'

'There's no need to apologise. Oh, I wish I knew what to do, Jane. Eddie and I've known each other since we were children. I care about him very much. He says he loves me, but—'

'But?'

'There are so many things I want to do – make a success of my career, travel, write. I'm not sure I'm ready to settle down.'

'All of those things sound like praiseworthy aims, my dear, and in the modern world, I believe one may not have to make such a stark choice.'

Rose smiled wanly. 'That's a comforting thought, thank you.'

Jane looked over to the gate that led from the drive. 'Ah, Shanti's back. We'll need another teacup.'

Rose laughed. 'Tea: the answer to everything.' She stood up. 'I'll go and meet him.'

CHAPTER 27

A price for the Morris Minor was agreed and not long afterwards, it was delivered to Sunnybank. On the afternoon of her first lesson, Jane sat in the driver's seat, listening carefully as Jayasena went through a lengthy explanation of how everything worked.

'If all that is clear, memsahib,' he said when he'd finished explaining, 'it is time to turn on the engine. But before you do so, please repeat for me what you need to be sure of first.'

Jane felt a little surge of excitement, although if she had been asked, she would have admitted that it was mingled with apprehension. 'That the handbrake is on, and I disengage the clutch by pressing down the pedal on the left.'

'Where should the right foot be?'

'On the brake pedal.'

'Very good, memsahib. And then after you have turned the engine on?'

'Put the stick into first gear and move my right foot to the accelerator. Press that down gently, at the same time lifting my left foot from the clutch.'

Jayasena beamed. 'We are ready to start.'

Jane frowned in concentration as she silently repeated the steps then began to carry them out. It all looked so easy when someone else was driving, she thought ruefully as her first effort ended with an abrupt jolt. Jayasena smiled patiently. 'Lift the foot a little more slowly from the clutch, memsahib.'

Jane bit her lip. 'I'll try.'

On her next attempt, the jolt was less alarming, and on the fourth try, the car moved smoothly forward over the gravel. She felt a surge of pride. 'I've done it, Jayasena!'

'Now you must practice stopping, memsahib.'

'But I've only just managed to start!'

'Sometimes, memsahib, it is more important to know how to stop.'

'I see your point.' Jane put her foot on the brake and the clutch pedal. 'Is that right?'

Jayasena chuckled. 'Yes, memsahib.'

'This time,' said Jane determinedly, 'I want to get into second gear.'

* * *

From the window in the hall, de Silva watched as the car moved forward once again, slowly gathering speed as it went down the drive. It would take time for him to get used to Jane at the wheel of a motor car but already he was less alarmed by the idea than he had been at first. One must move with the times, and he knew that whatever Jane set her mind to, she would do it well.

It was Saturday afternoon and he decided to relax and read until Jane returned from her lesson. In the drawing room he picked up the copy of Voltaire's *Candide* that he had been reading before the day of the Hill Country Cup. It wasn't such an easy read as his favourite P. G. Wodehouse novels, but it repaid the effort, and the story seemed particularly pertinent now that war had made the world a more dangerous place than it had been a few years ago.

On the verandah, he opened the book at the last page he had read. After Candide and his companions, Pangloss and Martin, had travelled the world encountering terrible perils and suffering, they had come to live on a small farm close to Constantinople where they heard news that a high-ranking official at the Ottoman Court had been murdered. Soon afterwards they met an old Turkish farmer and asked him what he'd heard about the news. He told them that in his view, people who meddled in politics usually met a miserable end, and indeed they deserved to. The old man never bothered with all that but spent his time tending to his garden and selling his produce.

Candide, on his way home, reflected deeply on what the farmer had said. He decided the old man was in a far happier place than kings and princes. '*I also know*,' he said to his companions, '*that we must cultivate our garden.*'

De Silva took off his reading glasses and paused to think about the words that Voltaire had written. There was comfort and hope in them. Despite the troubles of the world, happiness could be found in small endeavours and achievements. For example, it was there in the satisfaction he felt when he saw his flowers and vegetables flourish, and the figs and apricots on his trees ripen.

He looked over at Billy and Bella, dozing peacefully in the shade, and smiled. Lucky little creatures: they seemed to know instinctively how to unravel the secret of contentment. He put on his glasses once more and went back to his book.